P9-DYY-767

Exit Fee

Also by Brad Taylor

Daughter of War
Operator Down
Ring of Fire
Ghosts of War
The Forgotten Soldier
The Insider Threat
No Fortunate Son
Days of Rage
The Polaris Protocol
The Widow's Strike
Enemy of Mine
All Necessary Force
One Rough Man

Novellas
The Ruins
The Infiltrator
The Target
The Recruit
The Dig
Black Flag
Gut Instinct
The Callsign

Exit Fee

A Pike Logan Novella

BRAD TAYLOR

wm

WILLIAM MORROW IMPULSE

An Imprint of HarperCollinsPublishers

This is a work of fiction. Names, characters, places, and incidents are products of the author's imagination or are used fictitiously and are not to be construed as real. Any resemblance to actual events, locales, organizations, or persons, living or dead, is entirely coincidental.

Excerpt from *Hunter Killer* copyright © 2020 by Brad Taylor.

EXIT FEE. Copyright © 2019 by Brad Taylor. All rights reserved. Printed in the United States of America. No part of this book may be used or reproduced in any manner whatsoever without written permission except in the case of brief quotations embodied in critical articles and reviews. For information, address HarperCollins Publishers, 195 Broadway, New York, NY 10007.

Digital Edition OCTOBER 2019 ISBN: 978-0-06-298490-6
Print Edition ISBN: 978-0-06-298489-0

Cover design by Lisa Amoroso
Cover photographs © plainpicture/Mark Owen (man); © Henryk Sadura/Getty Images (buildings); © Kapustin Igor/Shutterstock (palm trees); © Avirut S/Shutterstock (clouds); © Petrov Stanislav/ Shutterstock (texture)

William Morrow Impulse is a trademark of HarperCollins Publishers.

William Morrow and HarperCollins are registered trademarks of HarperCollins Publishers in the United States of America and other countries.

FIRST EDITION

19 20 21 22 23   HDC   10 9 8 7 6 5 4 3 2 1

Author's Note

I CREATED AMENA knowing she probably wouldn't survive the trials in *Daughter of War*, but when it came time for her demise, I just couldn't do it. I liked her too much. But as always happens when I write—after putting my heart and soul into the story—I'm left with the question of "Now what?" Amena is the biggest "Now what?" of my writing career. I had intended for her to exit stage left in a neat and tidy bow, but decided against that. I now have to figure out a way for her to exist in the Pike Logan universe, and this novella is really my segue into this new reality—exploring Amena's relationship with Pike and Jennifer. I hope you enjoy!

Exit Fee

Chapter 1

PULLING UP TO the stoplight, Beth saw a girl her own age in the adjacent lane. She was young, attractive, and happy. She was just like Beth, except for the happiness part. That, and the fact that she had probably entered the Holy City of her own volition.

Beth looked at her across the lane, and saw her wave. Beth waved back, finding a connection that the girl would never understand. The girl began rolling down her window, and when Beth reached for her own, she heard, "Don't do it. Leave the window alone and shut the fuck up. Right now."

She turned and saw Slaven Kovac in the driver's seat next to her, glaring. A handsome man of about thirty-five, with close-cropped black hair, piercing green eyes, and a cleft chin, he was the one who'd groomed her online, and the only one of the three who could show moments of compassion. But she'd learned early that he was still capable of moments of pain. She shrank into her seat, and the light turned green. The car rolled on to the next stop of her life in hell.

She had done nothing to deserve this. She wasn't a heroin addict or a thief. She was just a child who'd made a bad decision. One her parents were trying desperately to unravel, with little luck. Coming from an upper-middle-class life in Colorado, they had no experience in such things. No idea of what to do or where to turn. They believed she had simply run away and were praying she would return of her own volition. They'd filed the requisite missing persons reports, stapled her picture all over their town, put up a reward, but clung to the belief that it was their daughter's choice not to come home. If they'd known the truth, it would have devastated them.

Their daughter had been sold into sexual slavery, something they simply could not fathom in their worst nightmares, which was a blessing for them, but not for Beth. As much as they'd fought to find their daughter, they were way behind the men who had taken her. Beth had been forced to give up her body for pay over and over, without any chance of escape. Unless she paid the exit fee to the men who held her.

But that price was more than she was willing to give, even with the hell she endured. Even as the other women in the stable told her it was the best choice. If she stayed, she'd eventually end up dead. The exit fee was her best option. But she couldn't bring herself to pay it.

The car rolled through the heart of Charleston, South Carolina, and she saw the families playing on the street. She saw herself from six months ago. She wished beyond anything to go home to Colorado. To forget about the fight she'd had with her mother. To forget about the time she crawled out of her window to physically meet the man she'd talked to online, Slaven Kovac. To reset her life.

She watched the people walking about, without a care in the world, and started to sob, keeping it quiet, to prevent a slap for her weakness.

She remembered reading Dante's *Inferno* her last year in high school, where she couldn't understand half of what her English teacher was trying to impart about the symbolism and meaning of the poem. Now she did, because she was living it.

Slaven said, "Cut that shit out. We're going to the house, and then you'll do just like before. I promise this time there will be no violence. Just you and a man. It's Charleston."

She nodded, knowing this town would be like all the others, but hoping he was telling the truth about the violence. They traveled down the cross-town, then took a left at a sign pointing the way to Folly Beach. Thirty minutes later, the car pulled up to a stoplight in the center of a small town, the streets lined with beach shops, bars, and restaurants. Slaven went right on Ashley Avenue, passing a seedy motel advertising single-use cottages. Slaven said, "That'll be your work area. Radovan said he's already used it with Misty the last two nights."

He slowed down and she saw a crumbling one-story building set back from the road, a small neon sign announcing, "Vacation Rentals—Vacancy." Behind it was a row of four small cottages, interspersed between garbage cans and cars, all of them looking like they'd been built in the sixties.

Slaven continued driving for another mile, the road lined with beach houses and old brick ranch dwellings. He eventually pulled into a circular drive in front of a two-story wooden house on stilts, the first floor ringed with a porch and a long stairwell leading to the front door.

He said, "This is home for the next week. Same rules as always."

She nodded, grabbed her small bag from the backseat, then followed behind him up the stairs, her head down. The door opened before he even knocked, and Beth saw Radovan Dragovic, the man the girls called the Enforcer. Broad-shouldered and tall, with a receding hairline and a thick, bony brow, he had pig eyes and a slit of a mouth that was perpetually open, showcasing teeth that looked too small for his gums. She'd been told that he'd had his nose smashed sometime in the past, and it hadn't healed correctly, leaving him a constant mouth breather. She instinctively hid behind Slaven, knowing that Radovan sometimes liked to slap the girls just for fun.

He shook Slaven's hand as they entered, and Beth wondered where the third man was. The one they called Doc. She caught herself searching the den and folded her head down, eyes on the floor, standing meekly waiting on instructions. She'd learned the best way to stay out of trouble was to try to remain invisible.

They began talking in a strange language she didn't understand, a guttural, coarse dialect they preferred to use with one another. After a brief conversation, Slaven turned to her with fake exuberance and said, "Hey, you have a repeat customer! Some guy from Virginia is down here in Charleston. He saw you on the website and you must have made an impression."

Virginia had been weeks ago, and the mention of the state was no help at all. The only good thing was that, precisely because she couldn't remember, nothing horrible had happened there. She most definitely remembered Washington, D.C.

She simply nodded. He said, "Go upstairs and find your room. This one is downtown, tonight. Looks like you get over with only one this time. Misty will have to pick up your slack with a full slate. Get out of those scuzzy shorts and put on the sundress I bought you. Clean up. I want you looking like a tourist. We'll go check out the venue. Make sure you know where to go."

Meaning, *Make sure you don't get any ideas about fleeing.*

She stood for a pregnant second, and Radovan snarled and raised his hand. She grabbed her bag, put her other arm over her head, and raced up the stairs, hearing him laugh behind her.

She opened a bedroom door and saw Misty on the bed, her right eye black, but her joy at Beth's arrival real. She jumped up and said, "About time! We've been here for three days."

Beth smiled back and said, "I know. I had a lineup in Myrtle Beach that Slaven wanted to take care of."

She said it like she was talking about pruning the bushes on a lawn, her life now nothing more than clawing for a day without pain. Misty took it the same way, grabbing Beth's bag and throwing it on the bed, chatting as if they were having a sleepover, but Beth caught an edge.

Misty said, "I've been working nights here, and have a lineup again tonight. So far, it hasn't been too bad. The motel is sleazy as hell, but the johns are all pretty normal."

Beth said, "I'm going downtown. Apparently, I have a repeat customer. Someone from Norfolk."

Misty smiled, the edge coming back, saying, "No kidding. Look at you go."

Beth misunderstood the reticence, saying, "I'm sorry, but that leaves you with the Enforcer."

Misty touched her eye and said, "Not your fault."

Beth looked around the room and said, "Where's Tess's stuff? Where's Tess?"

And she learned why Misty was on edge. "She's paying the exit fee."

Shocked, Beth said, "What? She said that would never happen."

"I know. She refused to work last night. It was the third time. Radovan forced her to pay. Doc is with her now, down the hall."

Beth sagged into the bed, the fake cheerfulness gone. She put her head into her hands and began to weep. Misty sat down next to her, rubbing her back, and then she began to cry as well.

They were jerked out of their emotional pain by Slaven yelling, "What's taking so fucking long? Get down here."

Beth leapt up, shouting, "I'm coming, I'm coming." She rapidly changed her clothes, touched up her makeup, and said, "I'll see you tonight. Don't pay the fee. Promise me that."

Misty nodded, and then said, "They'll be looking for someone to replace Tess."

"I know."

"Don't help them."

Beth grabbed her purse, turned, and said, "I won't. I promise," then raced down the stairs.

— *Chapter 2*

THIRTY MINUTES LATER, Slaven and Beth were in the heart of downtown Charleston, parking in a garage off Cumberland Street. They walked down to Church Street, and Slaven pointed out an Irish pub called Tommy Condon's. He said, "He'll meet you inside there tonight at 6 P.M. I'll be in the back, just to keep you safe."

Yeah, right.

They continued on and he pointed at a hotel next door called the French Quarter Inn, saying, "That's where he'll take you. The man certainly has money, so don't fuck this up. He's paying way more than the market rate for your ass."

And Beth remembered who the john was. Some sort of scientist with the U.S. Navy who had also paid for a first-rate hotel in Norfolk. A gentle man, actually. Someone who apparently thought what he was doing was romantic. She knew she'd get dinner out of the deal, along with a single partner on this night. Small blessings.

They rounded the corner onto Market Street, the place crowded with tourists darting in and out of the old brick slave market, and Slaven kept walking, circling around East Bay until they reached Vendue Range. He walked toward the water, stopping at an ice cream shop, a fountain at the end of the street with children dancing and playing inside the water and the Charleston harbor stretching out behind. He pulled up a chair at an outside table and said, "You got it?"

She nodded, and he said, "One other thing. This guy is a whale. I don't know why he seeks you out on the webpages, but he's got more to offer than just a lay. When you're in his room, get his information. I want to know who he is. We might be able to use that for some more revenue. He's rich, but keeping this secret, and we may want to leverage that."

She nodded again, thinking, *Aren't I enough? Now you want to destroy this guy's world as well?*

And then she thought of what she was being forced to do, and who was paying to make that happen. The man was the very reason there was a market for her. She snarled, "You got it."

Slaven caught the tone and laughed, saying, "Don't screw this up. Keep your phone on you. I don't like this setup. We don't control the venue, and it might be dangerous."

Even as she understood what the john represented, she knew he wasn't dangerous in the slightest, and that the phone Slaven had given her was slaved to his own, letting him see everything she texted, searched on the web, and even the numbers she called. She knew what he meant was, *You'll have an opportunity to flee, but if you do, you will be punished.*

She nodded again and said, "I understand, daddy."

He patted her hand, showing the same man he had been when he'd groomed her. "You're always the good one, Beth. I wouldn't let Tess or Misty do this, because they'd cause trouble, but you never do."

At the mention of Tess, she felt the despair return. She didn't want to show it, but she knew she was not going to live for another six months. Tess proved it. Even when they asked for the exit fee, if you didn't agree, they would just take it.

Nobody was ever going to help her. Not the johns she slept with, not the women in the stable, not anyone. She had prayed her parents would seek her out, but that hadn't happened. She'd prayed that someone would arrest the men who forced her to do the things she did, but that hadn't happened, either. She'd given up hope on anyone helping her.

She was but one of many women trapped in the sex trafficking trade, a business that occurred around the world, the women coming from all aspects of life. She had nobody and nothing on her side.

Well, she did have *one* thing.

She didn't know it yet, but she would have one experience that none of the other victims of the slave trade could duplicate. She met a refugee.

And that small child would bring more destruction than anything the men holding her could fathom.

Chapter 3

AMENA WAS BOUNCING off the cushions of our couch while waiting on us to get ready, shouting every five seconds, "What's taking so long, Pike? Let's gooooo."

In our bedroom, I finished tying my shoes, saw Jennifer in the bathroom brush something mysterious on her face, and decided to throw her under the bus. "It's not me. It's Jennifer."

Jennifer scowled at me, and I shrugged my shoulders, saying, "I'm ready."

I left the bedroom and found Amena in front of the TV, watching yet another *Game of Thrones* episode. She looked up and said, "We going to leave anytime soon?"

"Yes. But Jennifer's still doing her makeup. You should know about that."

She smiled and said, "Winter is coming. We need to go."

I chuckled at the phrase, because she had really dived headfirst into the series. She'd taken an extreme interest in one character—Arya—seeing herself in the young woman's story.

A child who'd been left on her own in that medieval world, Arya ended up becoming an assassin, defending herself when no one else seemed to care, and that was really Amena's story. Right down to the killing.

Amena was a Syrian refugee who had crossed our path on an operation in Europe, and she'd proven very resourceful. So much so, I'd decided to bring her to the United States, not the least because her actions had helped me stop a deadly chemical weapons attack. At first it had seemed idyllic, me the savior giving her the chance at a better life, but lately it had grown a little tense.

Like a stray cat who enjoyed being out of the weather when you open the door, but ultimately starts scratching the walls to get back outside, Amena had initially loved staying in our home, but eventually, she felt cooped up, demanding to be allowed to roam the streets of Charleston like she had in Europe.

I couldn't allow that, not because I was afraid for her—Lord knew she could take care of herself—but because she had no legal paperwork allowing her to be in the United States. Any incident involving the authorities would bring questions that neither she nor I could answer. And it really didn't have to be an incident, because her looks alone demanded attention. She was exotic, to say the least, with hazel eyes, black hair, and tanned skin. Even at the ripe old age of thirteen, people would stare and ask where she was from.

Because of the attention, I didn't let her go out on her own. Not until I could get her legal paperwork through some contacts I had. So far, that was taking much longer than I had expected, and now, four months later, she was growing tired of being on a leash.

It wasn't like I locked her up all day. I mean, she came with me to the store, and went with Jennifer on errands, but we didn't let her go out on her own. It was too big of a risk, but lately it had caused Amena to start fighting back, chafing at the restrictions, to the point where we argued more than we bonded.

I hated it and was glad she wasn't pushing the fight today.

I said, "Winter isn't coming here, I'll tell you that. It's damn near ninety degrees outside. You sure you want to walk to the market?"

She smiled and said, "Oh yeah. I'm sick of just riding in your car."

We lived off of East Bay, about a ten-minute walk from Market Street, and we'd promised to take her there today and let her run around a little bit. The Spoleto Festival was in town this week, and the area promised to be full of tourists who loved the arts. Something I just couldn't wait to join.

I said, "Yeah, you'll probably want to go home as soon as you see all the jackasses who've descended on our fair city. Jennifer, however, will force us to go look at some froufrou paintings."

I saw Amena's eyes widen, and realized Jennifer was standing behind me. Without missing a beat, I said, "But that artwork is really special, so I don't mind."

I heard Jennifer grunt, then turned around in mock surprise and said, "Hey, you ready to go?"

She said, "I'm not so sure."

Amena took it seriously and jumped up, saying, "He meant it. He wants to see the art. Don't stay here. Come with us."

Jennifer laughed, draped her arms over my shoulder, and kissed me on the cheek, saying, "I wouldn't miss it for the world."

Amena beamed, racing to the front door. Jennifer leaned into my ear and whispered, "You keep that up with her, and you'll regret it tonight."

All innocent, I said, "What? What did I do?"

She latched her teeth onto my earlobe, gave it a little nip, and said, "Be on your best behavior."

I said, "I can't do any less with you in the mix."

Amena was in the doorway, waiting. She said, "Come on!"

We both chuckled at her eagerness and followed her out the door.

Ten minutes later, Jennifer and I were sweating on a bench in Waterfront Park, the Charleston harbor behind us, while Amena splashed with other children in a large fountain, laughing and squealing.

I said, "You know we have to figure this out sooner rather than later. She's taking on an edge, and I honestly don't blame her. She's starting to fight me on everything."

Jennifer took my hand and said, "She just wants to be a child. She wants to be American. She doesn't understand your concern. I think she believes you're ashamed of her."

That took me by surprise. "What? Why on earth would you say that, after all we've done for her? I've explained to her—"

And she cut me off. "It's not about the words. It's about the deeds. She has no friends, she isn't enrolled in school, we don't let her out on her own. It just builds up in her mind."

"Are you serious?"

"Unfortunately, yes. We know we mean well, but put yourself in her shoes. She's had a traumatic life. Her entire family has been killed, with her brother and father slaughtered right in front of her. We don't let her do anything, and yes, you've told her why, but I don't think she believes it. Trust isn't something she's willing to give right now."

I took that in, then said, "So what do we do?"

"Maybe we give her a little more room. I know it's a risk, but we can take baby steps here."

Before I could answer, Amena came running up, her clothing damp from jumping under the spouts of water. She pointed up the road and said, "The kids in the fountain said there's an Italian ice cart up there."

I stood and said, "Yeah, those things are all over the city. Come on. I'll take you."

She pushed me back into the bench and said, "No. I want to go by myself."

I looked at Jennifer, and she gave me an imperceptible nod. I gave Amena a ten-dollar bill and said, "Okay, but bring me back a blue raspberry. And keep your phone on you."

She grinned, snatched the money out of my hand, and took off running down the right side of Vendue Range. I stood and shouted, "It's on the left side!" But she didn't hear me.

I sat back down, my eyes on her fleeing form, and Jennifer said, "Baby steps."

Amena stopped at a table outside of an ice cream shop, apparently asking for directions. The next thing I knew, she sat down with the people at the table. I tensed up, and Jennifer said, "What?"

"She's talking to someone."

At the table was a young woman of about sixteen or eighteen and an older man. He was too young to be her father, but much too old to be a date. He gave off a weird vibe. I leaned forward, causing Jennifer to say, "What?"

"Nothing. Just watching."

She followed my eyes, and said, "Maybe she decided on ice cream instead of Italian ice."

I said, "Maybe so." And then we both watched Amena rise, skipping farther down the avenue before she was lost to the crowds.

Jennifer said, "Doesn't look like anything bad happened."

"Maybe. Maybe not. But that guy isn't an angel."

She laughed and said, "Because he looks a little rough? Have you checked a mirror lately?"

She had a point about the mirror. I wouldn't win any modeling contracts unless they were looking for a pirate. With a scar that tracked all the way from my eyebrow to my lower cheek, I was the guy on the street you instinctively looked away from for fear of pissing me off. But that wasn't what I meant. The man was actually good-looking in a foreign sort of way, but he was giving off a vibe I didn't like. But maybe that was just my overprotective instincts kicking in.

I said, "I'm not talking about his looks."

She gave me a sidelong glance, but said nothing. I caught sight of Amena coming back down the road on the opposite side of the man at the table, trying to eat her Italian ice while carrying mine. It brought a smile to my face.

She reached us and gave me my blue raspberry, then slid in next to Jennifer. I said, "Change?"

She said, "That's my tip for going to get it."

I let it slide, asking, "Who was the man you were talking to?"

"I wasn't talking to the man. I was talking to the girl. She's new here too."

"Well, be careful what you tell them. We've talked about this."

I saw the anger building and held up my hands, saying, "I'm just trying to protect you."

She said, "No, you're not. You're trying to keep me locked up. So what if I talked to them? What's the big deal? What are you afraid of? Me learning my way around and not needing you anymore?"

I said, "Amena, that's not it at all. I'm just trying to keep you safe until you have the required paperwork."

And without even meaning to, I set off some sort of time bomb. She jumped off the bench, saying, "What you want is to keep me under your thumb. I've been here for four months and all I do is sit in your apartment. I'm sick of that."

I looked at Jennifer and said, "Whoa, there. That's not fair."

She pulled out the phone I'd given her, tossed it into my lap, and said, "I'm going exploring."

I stood up. "No, you're not. Amena, stop this. I'll call my people again. See if I can speed things up, but you're not going running around on your own."

She went from me to Jennifer, then said, "Yes, I am, and you're not stopping me, unless you want me to start screaming that I've been kidnapped. Which I practically have been."

My eyes about popped out of my head. I said, "Jenn?"

Jennifer said, "Amena, I know you're frustrated, but Pike is right here."

She said, "I'm going exploring. *Without* you two. I'll be home later."

And just like that, she took off running back up the avenue. I stood there with my mouth open for a second, looked at Jennifer, then started to follow. Jennifer shouted, "Pike!"

I turned, and she said, "Let her go. She'll be home tonight, and when she comes home, we'll have a heart-to-heart. Let her get some of it out of her system."

"But what if she gets into trouble? She doesn't even have her phone. There's no way we can help her."

Jennifer said, "How much trouble can she get into in Charleston?"

Chapter 4

AMENA SPRINTED DOWN the street, waiting on Pike to snatch her collar. She felt nothing and slowed to a walk, glancing behind her. She saw him standing up next to Jennifer, but he made no move to catch her.

So he really doesn't care.

As much as she fought him, she wanted to believe in him. Wanted to believe that he loved her for who she was. That what he said was true, and he was keeping her in a cage because it was the best for her.

She stopped next to a store selling tourist flotsam for the cruise ships that came and went, watching him sit back down, the visitors swirling around her. Like she had in the past, she judged the ebb and flow of patrons, and realized she could blend in here just like she had in Monaco. Easier, even.

If Pike didn't want to chase her, she could make it on her own. She'd done it for years. She turned to go and felt a tug deep in her heart. A yearning not to leave.

Come for me. Please come chase me.

She saw Jennifer lead Pike away from the fountain, holding hands. It broke her heart.

She watched them disappear behind a building, her anchor in this world shrinking with every step, and made a childish decision. She couldn't be faulted for that. She was, after all, a child.

She glanced down the street and saw the same girl who'd given her directions earlier. She walked at a crisp pace until she was next to her.

The girl looked up, surprised. Amena sat down and said, "Where's your friend?"

"He's inside. Getting some ice cream. What are you doing here?"

"I can do what I want. I don't need permission."

The girl glanced at the front of the store and said, "You need to leave. Get out of here. You don't want anything to do with us. Please."

The comment confused Amena. She said, "I thought you guys were visiting here like I was?"

"We are, but we don't want anything to do with you."

Taken aback at the hostility, Amena said, "Why were you so friendly before? What did I do?"

The girl leaned in and hissed, "Get the fuck away from this table."

Amena stood and felt a hand on her shoulder. She turned and saw the man from before. He said, "Hey, what's going on here, Beth? A little catfight?"

Beth ducked her head, the hostility gone. She said, "No, nothing like that. She said she needed to get home."

Amena said, "That's not true. I can stay for a little bit."

The man sat down and said, "Before your family starts looking?"

Amena sat down next to him, unaware of the danger. "I have no family. They're gone."

"What's that mean?"

Amena remembered what Pike had told her, and said, "Nothing. Just that I don't have any immediate family."

The man said, "My name is Slaven, and I think we are more alike than you know. I'm from Bosnia, and I lost my family in war. I never got over it."

Amena heard the words and felt a kinship. He was like her. She said, "I lost my family in Syria. How did your family die?"

He rolled his head back, looking at the sky, and said, "They died because they were in the wrong place at the wrong time. Nothing else."

He came back to her and said, "And your family?"

She hesitated, then said, "The same thing. The exact same thing. Where in Bosnia are you from?"

"Do you know it?"

She leaned back, embarrassed. "No. Not really. I was in France once, but I don't know Bosnia."

He grinned and said, "That's okay. I'm from a small town called Zvornik, in the Republic of Sprska. A spit of land that is attacked daily in the press for no reason. Have you heard of it?"

Amena said, "No, but I've learned that most people in this world don't understand the fight that happens outside of their view."

The girl grabbed Amena's hand and said, "You're right about that. You are *right* about that. Maybe it's time you went home."

Slaven put a hand on Beth's shoulder and she shut down. He said, "You want to go with us to Folly Beach? We have a house there on the water. You want to come?"

Amena thought about it, and said, "Can you bring me back? I don't have a car."

"Of course. I'll bring you right back here."

Beth said, "I don't think that's a good idea. You should probably go home."

Amena looked at her and saw pain. Slaven put a hand on Beth's shoulder and said, "One more would be fun, I think."

For the first time, Amena felt a sliver of danger. She said, "Maybe it's not a good idea. I don't want to intrude."

Slaven turned on a hundred-watt smile and said, "You're not intruding. We came here for a vacation. You'll enjoy it, unless you're worried about your family coming to find you."

Amena glanced back down the avenue, seeing the empty bench. She said, "I don't have a family."

Slaven said, "Then we'll be your new family. Isn't that right, Beth?"

Beth forced a smile and said, "Yes, it'll be fun. It's the beach."

Amena nodded, banishing her nascent fear. If Pike didn't want to spend time with her, she would find her own friends. She stood and followed them to a parking garage, reaching a beat-up Toyota Corolla. Slaven opened the door and said, "You hungry? You want some food before we go? It's about thirty minutes away."

The generosity was a soothing lullaby to Amena. What bad person would offer to buy her lunch after just meeting? She said, "Nope. I'd rather see the beach."

Slaven nodded, and she slid into the seat in the back next to Beth. She spent the drive answering question after question from Slaven. Not wanting to get Pike in trouble, Amena spouted out answers that carved out a space around both Pike and Jennifer. As far as Slaven knew, she was on her own in Charleston.

Eventually, they pulled up to a clapboard beach house with a balcony surrounding it, the Atlantic Ocean spilling out to the horizon behind it. Amena opened the door and said, "This is beautiful."

Slaven smiled, then said something confusing. "Beth, since Amena's here, you'll be going on your own tonight. Is that going to be a problem?"

Beth said, "No. I understand."

"Be sure and take your phone. I'll be checking."

She nodded, and Amena followed them up the stairs to the porch, wanting to ask Beth what that meant. The door opened, and she saw a man who looked straight out of *Game of Thrones*. Tall, at least six-foot-five, he had a receding hairline and a face that broadcast cruelty.

In Serbian, he said, "Who's that?"

Slaven said, "Maybe a replacement. She's our guest."

The man nodded, and Amena stumbled on the stairs at his appearance and the unfamiliar language, seeking purchase with her feet going back down. Slaven caught her and laughed, saying in English, "Hey, don't break your leg."

Amena just looked at him, her gut instinct inside telling her to flee.

Slaven turned on the smile and said, "Come on. We have sandwich stuff. And then we can go to the beach."

She tentatively nodded and followed him into the house. Slaven said, "Beth, you don't have a lot of time. Go take a shower and get ready."

Amena said, "She can't come to the beach with me?"

"She can later. She's got to get ready for work. Come on, I'll make you a sandwich."

Beth went upstairs and Amena followed him into the kitchen, seeing the expanse of Folly Beach outside the window. Hesitantly, trying to regain the camaraderie of the car ride, she said, "This is really pretty."

Slaven said, "Radovan, get me some bread from the pantry."

The cruel man did as he asked without a word. The entire sequence was putting Amena on edge. She said, "I have to use the bathroom."

A knife in his hand, cutting up a tomato, Slaven pointed with the edge and said, "Go up to Beth's room."

She did so and heard sobbing coming from a bedroom as she walked up the stairs. She stopped and listened, hearing Beth talking about an exit fee, another woman in pain, then talking about her. She entered, finding Beth sitting on the closed toilet in the rear of the bedroom, crying, another woman above her rubbing her shoulders. They saw her appear and jumped up.

Amena said, "What's wrong?"

The other woman looked over Amena's shoulder in fear, like someone might be behind her, then said, "Nothing. Nothing's wrong."

Amena squinted her eyes and said, "Something's wrong. What was that about another woman? Is someone hurt?"

The woman glanced toward the hallway, trying mightily to remain calm. "No. Really, no."

Amena followed her eyes, glancing behind her, then said, "Is she in the other room?"

Beth jumped up and said, "No! She's not."

And that was enough. Amena backed up, holding her hands in front of her, wondering what she had entered. She reached the hallway and saw another door farther down. She went to it, put her hand on the door-knob, and Beth reached her, saying, "You need to go. Now. While you still can."

Amena opened the door and saw a woman on a bed, ghostly pale, with an intravenous drip above her head, the tube ending in a vein just below her biceps. On her abdomen was an angry red wound, the stitching haphazard, like someone unskilled had done it.

She turned to flee and ran headlong into Slaven.

He said, "Little one, you could have had a few good days here before I put you to work. Why did you go exploring?"

Chapter 5

LANNISTER MCBRIDE CHECKED the clock and saw it was closing in on 5 P.M. It would take him about thirty minutes to get from the Naval Weapons Station at Goose Creek to downtown Charleston. He still had some work to do and thought maybe he should have selected a later time to meet.

A civilian subcontractor working at the Naval Nuclear Power Training Command, he was partially responsible for the quality control of the two nuclear-powered submarines that the students used as training vehicles. A graduate of the Naval Nuclear Power School himself, he'd served twenty-one years in the navy, on both nuclear aircraft carriers and nuclear submarines.

He had to be close to the Naval Weapons Station and because of that, unlike at the navy base at Norfolk, he was far removed from the action of downtown Charleston. Norfolk was a navy town, and as such, it catered to the military. Charleston used to be that way, but in one of the multitude of base realignment closures during the Clinton years, Charleston had lost its naval base— and with it, the distinction that the Norfolk Naval Base still held.

Once the largest port of nuclear submarines in the United States, the Charleston Naval Base had shrunk down to the Charleston Naval Weapons Station, becoming an appendage of crumbling warehouses and shuttered buildings that were slowly being taken over by hipster breweries and flea markets. The only thing left of note was the Nuclear Power School, but there was no support on the base anymore. No hospitals, no commissaries, no base exchange, no feeling of being on a military base at all. They didn't even have any on-base housing for people like him anymore, forcing Lannister to stay at a long-term hotel outside of the gate. The final nail in the coffin had come when the command for the navy had merged with the Charleston Air Force Base, becoming "Joint Base Charleston," with the naval forces now holding an office building at an air force installation, of all places.

Even with all of that, Charleston had its perks.

Lanny was happily married, with a wife and a nice ranch house in Hampton Roads, Virginia, and that happiness came from the fact that he was always on the road. They both loved each other, but neither had realized how much being deployed at sea with the navy had factored into their relationship. One year after retiring, they were completely sick of each other and on the verge of a divorce, then he'd found this contracting job. He traveled for months on end, just like he was still in the navy, and like those deployments, he carved out time to find some local girls for friendship.

He'd become accustomed to using the ubiquitous sex site BackPage.com, but that was shuttered by federal agents in 2018. Since then, he'd been shopping around, trying to find the next BackPage, and had landed on a site called Skipthegames. The webpage was located in Europe, but had plenty of ads for the United States, including Charleston, and it also had the added benefit of pictures. He'd perused it last night and was surprised to see a girl listed that he'd been with in Norfolk. Beth something-or-other.

She'd been sweet, and while she'd claimed to be eighteen, he was pretty sure she was younger. Just like the women he'd found in the old days of port liberty in Thailand and the Philippines. He'd used the webpage to book her for a night, but he didn't want her to come here, right next to the naval base, so he'd made a reservation downtown at a swanky place called the French Quarter Inn.

He reviewed the instructions he'd been sent one more time, did a Google Map check of Tommy Condon's, then packed up a go-bag with fresh underwear, toothbrush and toothpaste, a condom, and a cheap bouquet of flowers he'd purchased at a grocery store. He checked himself in the mirror, slapped his gut as if that would make it disappear, and then left his spartan room for the one downtown.

He spent the drive thinking about what he would do with the night. At the end of the day, he fully understood he was paying for sex, but he liked to pretend—at least in his own mind—that it was a date. He hadn't had that in the Philippines, and it had made him feel dirty, like an exploiter of women. Something he had never liked.

Now, with the money he made on his contracts, whenever he ordered women, he didn't just sleep with them and leave. He made it into an affair that lasted the night, including dinner, drinks, and a nice hotel room. He knew it was false, but it kept him from the slimy notion of being a john in a back alley. He was better than that. Noble.

He pulled into the parking garage on Cumberland Street, picked up the flowers and his go-bag from the passenger seat, locked up, and went down the stairwell to the entrance of the garage, a grin slipping out even as he tried to contain it.

He reached a landing and another man entered the stairwell, his face grim. Lannister glanced up and saw a bright scar tracking down through his brow and into his cheek, giving the man the look of death. Lannister ducked his head and went by him, not wanting to give the passerby any reason to engage him. He failed to realize he'd just passed the instrument of his own destruction.

Chapter 6

IT WAS CLOSING in on 5 P.M. and Amena hadn't come home. Jennifer was now pacing the house like a caged panther. She finally looked at me and said, "Okay, we need to find her. Before it gets dark."

I was glad her idea about giving Amena a little freedom was wearing off, because I was really starting to worry.

She'd run off into the crowd over five hours ago and hadn't shown back up at our house. We both thought she'd be gone for an hour or two, max, but that hadn't happened. Deep down, I knew something wasn't right, and I felt the blame in my soul. I should have stopped her. Should have been the parent I once was.

I said, "I'll go drive around the market and see if I can find her. It'll be okay. She's probably back in the fountain."

Jennifer said, "Get the Taskforce on this. Find her phone."

I held up Amena's handset and said, "She left her phone. I can't even track it."

Jennifer slapped the counter and said, "I swear, when I get my hands on that child . . ."

I grinned, and then saw a tear form in her eye. I said, "Hey, I'll go get her. It's not going to end badly."

She said, "She might have run away for real. Don't let her go. Please. We brought her here. Promised her things. And now she's going to end up in a ditch."

I said, "Cut that out. She isn't going to run away. If anything, she's running around Charleston fleecing the tourists."

Jennifer bored into me and said, "That's not it. You know it. You feel it. I can see it in your eyes."

And she was right. Amena touched me in a way that I hadn't felt since my daughter had died. We had a connection, and that connection was telling me something was bad. But I didn't want Jennifer to believe it was her fault for letting Amena go. And she most definitely felt that way.

I said, "I'll go circle downtown. See what I can see."

She said, "I'm coming with you."

"No. You're not. She might come home. Someone needs to be here. Let me do this alone."

She looked at me with unadulterated pain and said, "Why did I let her run off?"

I leaned in and kissed her, saying, "It wasn't you. What you did was right. What happened after isn't your fault. I'll find her."

She took the kiss, then leaned back, looking at me with a ferocious stare. She said, "Get her back here. Do what you do."

I said, "I will. In the meantime, stay by your phone. She might call you for a ride."

I exited our house at a trot, jogging down the stairs to my dented Jeep CJ-7. It wasn't as comfortable as Jennifer's Mini Cooper, but it was certainly recognizable, which is something I wanted in case Amena was looking for us.

I wanted to believe that, but knew if that were the case, she would have just walked home.

I cut over to King Street, rode that down to Broad Street, then circled back up East Bay, cutting down Market, then circling to the fountain on Vendue Range. I saw nothing but tourists. No sign of Amena. I decided to go on foot, driving up Cumberland to the parking garage. I found a spot on the third floor, started walking down the stairwell, and saw a man on the level below me exit a Hyundai carrying a cheap bouquet of flowers, a small knapsack on his back. He reached the stairwell just as I rounded the floor above and glanced away. Which was something I was used to. I let him go in front, me four steps above him, and he picked up his pace like he didn't want me behind him. Something else I was used to.

By the time I broke out into the sunshine, he was at the door to an old Irish pub called Tommy Condon's. He entered, and I went left, back to Market Street, my head on a swivel looking for Amena.

Forty-five minutes later, I was walking back to my car, dreading the call I would have to make to Jennifer. She hadn't called me, so I knew there had been no activity at home. I rounded the corner of Cumberland Street and saw the bouquet guy walking with a female. I did a double take when I saw her.

It was the girl that Amena had talked to at the ice cream shop. The older man I'd seen with her earlier was nowhere to be found. Just the flower boy and her. They disappeared into a brick tunnel leading to a building and I picked up my pace, wanting to ask the girl if she'd seen Amena.

I reached the tunnel and saw it was the entrance to a boutique hotel, one of many that dotted the peninsula of Charleston. I entered an atrium, swiveled my head around, but didn't see the couple. In front of me were a winding staircase leading up and a Ruth's Chris steakhouse that had just opened. I jogged forward and stuck my head in, seeing it deserted at this hour, with only a couple of businessmen at the bar. Staircase it was.

I sprinted up it, reached the hotel lobby area, and outdoor deck to the left. Once again I didn't see my targets. I went to the woman at the reception desk and said, "There was a man and a girl that just came in here. Did you see where they went?"

She pointed and said, "The elevator. They're staying here."

I nodded, started to move that way, and knew it wouldn't do me any good. I had no idea what floor they were on. I turned back around and said, "Look, I know your answer is going to want to be no, but I'm trying to find a lost child, and I think they might have seen her. Can you tell me what room they're in?"

She looked uncomfortable, but then gave the answer I knew was coming. "I'm sorry, sir, but I can't do that. I can, however, call the police for you."

With Amena's status, that was an absolute nonstarter. But I had a better idea. I said, "That's okay. It's not a crisis yet. I'll try another way."

She nodded, a little concern in her eyes, and I said, "Thanks anyway."

I left the lobby at a trot, running back down the stairs and pulling out my cell phone. I speed walked to the Cumberland parking garage dialing a number. When it answered, I heard, "Pike, hey, how are you?"

Threaded in between the salutation was a little dread. Because I never called this guy direct unless I had a problem, and usually what I wanted was illegal. Like now.

I said, "Hey, Creed, I've got a little issue here and could use some help."

"Pike, no, no, no. I'm not doing any hacking for you off the books."

I entered the stairwell for the garage, sprinted up to

the third floor, and said, "It's not a hack. It's just some data mining."

Bartholomew Creedwater was what respectable people called a computer network operations engineer. Which was like calling a whore a sexual therapist, because he was a hacker. He worked for the Taskforce and was very good at his job. He was my go-to guy for any official work that I needed to be accomplished—and he'd been willing to bend a law or two on my behalf in the past.

He said, "Pike, no way. I can't do it. It'll be logged and recorded. I'll get barbecued for breaking the law."

The Taskforce had a healthy offensive capability to use the cyber realm to solve counterterrorism threats, but that came with some rules to prevent it from running amok—the primary one being we weren't allowed to target any U.S. entities. On the surface, it seemed like we were "fighting with one arm tied behind our back," but that wasn't really true. Liberty needed protection as much as physical life, and I didn't mind the strictures. Honestly, having the capability was the same as having a rifle. Issued to me by the U.S. government, I could use it against the enemy all day long, but to take it out of the arms room and start shooting Americans on the street would be a nonstarter. It was no different with the new world of cyber collection capabilities.

But now, I needed his help, and he was the only one who could do it.

I exited onto the third deck and said, "I'm not asking you to do any hacking. Just give me a name from a database. I'm going to give you a license plate, and I need a name."

He said, "Pike, I can't do that. We're restricted from doing anything on U.S. soil. You know that."

I said, "Pretend I'm not on U.S. soil. Get me the name of the guy that owns this car."

"Pike . . . why?"

I reached the car and snarled, "Because I've lost Amena, and this fuck might be someone who knows where she is. That's why."

Amena had become a flashpoint in the Taskforce, precisely because I'd broken protocol to bring her to the United States, but Creed knew what she meant to me, and, unlike the other shits in the hierarchy, he actually cared.

I heard nothing for a moment, then, "Send it to me."

I took a picture of the license plate, sent it, then said, "Tell me who owns it."

A minute later, he said, "It's a rental. Hertz."

I said, "Who rented it?"

"Pike! That's going to take offensive action to figure out. I'm not searching static databases anymore."

I said, "Uh huh. Yeah. Answer the question. Who rented it?"

"Pike. I can't do that."

"Yes, you can. Look, I think Amena is in serious trouble. She's been gone for over five hours. This guy is with a woman who was with her. All I want to do is talk to him. That's all."

"Have you talked to Kurt about this?"

Kurt Hale was the commander of Project Prometheus—the official title for what we knuckle-draggers called the Taskforce—and of course I hadn't talked to him. I didn't need to. He'd done the same thing once saving his niece and had asked me to help him then. But I knew he'd tell me no here.

I said, "Just tell me who rented that car. That's all I'm asking."

I heard nothing for a moment, then: "It's a guy named Lannister McBride. He rented the car two weeks ago, with a return three weeks from now. Can I be done?"

Because of the speed with which I got the information, I knew he'd been working it before I even asked. He trusted me, and it meant a great deal.

I said, "Yeah, you can. Thank you."

Chapter 7

I NOW HAD a name, but had to figure out how to leverage it for offensive action. I called Jennifer. "Any word?"

"No, Pike, I haven't heard anything."

"Well, get your ass down to the Cumberland parking lot. I have a thread, but I can't do it by myself."

"What do you mean?"

"Just get down here. I need eyes on a vehicle, and a Demon Seed tracker. Something that works with the cell network. I have a car I want tracked. I'll explain when you get here."

Because she was who she was, she didn't even question me. She said, "On the way," and hung up.

I then sat for a minute against Lannister's car, leaning back and thinking about the call I was going to make. I needed to talk to the girl, but I had no idea about her name. That was okay, because all I really needed was to get her on the phone.

I decided that just plowing forward was the best bet. Make the call and be honest. If the two were on the up-and-up, he'd probably hand the phone to her, and I'd get my interview. If not, at least I'd be shaking the tree for Jennifer to exploit.

Which, in retrospect, was probably not the best idea, because even given all the evil I'd seen in the world, I had no idea that it had penetrated my own hometown and taken my little refugee.

I rang the number for the hotel and said, "Lannister McBride's room, please."

I waited a bit, and then someone answered.

"Hello?"

"Lannister McBride?"

"Yes."

"Hey, this is going to seem a little weird, but you're up there with a girl who was with my daughter. She's now gone, and I'm trying to find her. Could I talk to her, please?"

I heard breathing, then, "What the fuck are you talking about? I'm not up here with anyone. How did you get my name?"

And I realized he was doing something bad. The girl wasn't a relative or friend. She was a whore.

I said, "Hey, calm down. I'm just trying to find my daughter. That's all. Don't go crazy here. Can I talk to the woman you're with? Please? I don't care what you're doing."

He screamed, "I'm not with a woman!"

And the phone disconnected.

I tapped my cell in my hand, then redialed, asking for his room again. This time, nobody answered. I went to the edge of the parking garage to a vantage point where I could keep an eye on the front door of the hotel. I saw plenty of people coming and going, but thankfully not my target. I tapped my foot impatiently, like that would make Jennifer arrive faster. I heard a car circling up the floors and saw Jenn's little Mini Cooper rise up. I waved my hand and she pulled up next to me, saying, "What do you have?"

"I don't know. Maybe nothing, but there's a guy that went into the French Quarter Inn with the girl that Amena sat down next to, at the ice cream shop. I called his room and he clammed up. I want to know where he goes. He's our only contact with the woman, and we don't have the manpower to cover all the exits to catch her. They might be running out a back exit right now—but eventually he'll *have* to return to this car."

She squinted and said, "How did you call him on the phone?"

I tilted my head and she said, "Okay, okay, I won't ask. Where's his car?"

I pointed at the Hyundai four spots away and said, "Get the Demon Seed on it, and then get ready to follow.

Station at the exit. Pay your parking fee and wait. You'll get a thirty-minute grace period before you have to exit. He'll be out before then."

"Why do you think that?"

"Because he's spooked. I could hear it in his voice. I don't think he's staying here. I think he got a room for the night only, and now he's going to want to get back to his house."

"What if you're wrong?"

"Then we let the Demon Seed do its work. He'll leave sooner or later, and we won't need to do some *Starsky and Hutch* stakeout to see him exit. Put a geo-fence on this garage and when he breaks it, we're in business."

"What are you going to do?"

"Once you're set, I'm going to make another lap looking for Amena, but I don't think I'll see her. I want to brace this guy, but I want you to do it. I had contact with him in the stairwell here, so I don't want to spook him. You'll give him a sense of security because you're a female. I want you to get him to open up. I'll be right behind you, standing by if there's any trouble."

She said, "What's he got to do with Amena? Is it just the connection at the fountain?"

I shook my head, and she saw the pain. I said, "I know it sounds thin, but it's all we have right now. I honestly don't know if it has anything at all to do with Amena. But I *feel* it."

I looked at her, waiting on her to tell me this was crazy but needing her to continue, knowing I had no firm evidence that would penetrate her logical world. All I had was a feeling.

She smiled, saying, "That's good enough for me."

She put in a Bluetooth earpiece, flipped her cell phone over to our encrypted push-to-talk mode, and said, "Check, check."

I said, "Koko, got you lima charlie," then gave her a thumbs-up. I grinned when she scowled at her callsign, then watched her drive down the lane until she was behind the Hyundai. She glanced around, then rolled out, scooting underneath the back bumper. She spent about thirty seconds on the ground getting the Demon Seed and its antenna emplaced, then swiftly rolled back out, brushing off her shorts and climbing back into her car.

I saw her fiddle with a tablet, then heard, "It's set. Geo-fence is active."

The Demon Seed was a pretty simple tracker that used the digital LTE cell network to transmit locational data to her tablet with a plus or minus of ten meters. With a battery life of four days, we'd be able to know our target's every move without having to wrap him up like a wet blanket.

I returned my view to the front of the hotel and said, "Roger that. Go ahead and stage. I'm going to take another lap, see if I can spot our little refugee."

No sooner had the words come out of my mouth than I saw Lannister McBride exit the hotel, walking rapidly toward the garage like he was trying to squeeze back a bout of diarrhea, his face squinting, his bouquet of flowers long gone.

I said, "Koko, Koko, target inbound. My car's a level above. Target's going unsighted because I can't have him make contact with me again. Go ahead and exit and let the beacon do its work."

"Roger all. What's the endstate here?"

"Find his bed down, then wring him out. The endstate is to locate and interrogate that girl."

Chapter 8

BETH EXITED THE Uber ride, not wanting to advance up the steps, but she knew she had no choice. Something had screwed up the biggest whale she'd ever had, and she didn't know what that was. She knew whatever answer she gave to Slaven and the Enforcer wouldn't be enough.

The whale, Lannister, had hung up the phone and demanded to know what nefarious thing she was doing in Charleston. She'd said she had no idea what he was talking about, and he'd asked about a girl she'd met. The one by the fountain.

She knew whom he was referring to, but didn't let on. She'd told him she knew nothing about a girl, and he'd stormed out, saying he wasn't going to be part of a criminal enterprise.

She'd watched him leave, then had sat in the hotel room for close to an hour, not wanting her easy night to be destroyed. She'd considered faking it and sleeping in the room, but she knew that, eventually, Slaven would ask for the money. Money she didn't have. Finally, she'd taken the Uber back to Folly Beach, worried about what she would experience. In truth, she worried about the girl the man had mentioned. She knew where the girl was being held, because it was her own personal prison. She felt guilt in her soul about her inability to protect the little girl, knowing she would now experience the same thing Beth had.

She walked up the stairs, the light from the summer sun fading and giving the house a magical patina that was perfect for an Instagram post, but she didn't feel the magic. She turned the knob and found it locked. She held her fist over the wood, not wanting to step into the wrath she knew was coming.

She rapped the door, once, twice, three times. And then stood with her head down.

Radovan opened the door, seeing her cowering, and gave no comfort. He said, "Why are you here so soon?"

She said, "I have to talk to Slaven."

He smacked her cheek hard enough to knock her into the door frame and said, "Why?"

She held her arms over her head and said, "Slaven. Slaven."

He huffed, disgusted. He grabbed her by her head and hoisted her into the foyer, spilling her onto the floor.

She cowered, and then heard Slaven's voice. She looked up and saw him above her.

He said, "What did you do?"

"Nothing. I did nothing. I went to the bar like you asked. I went to the room like you asked. I was doing what you wanted, and the phone rang. He answered it, and it was the end of the date."

"Why? Who was calling?"

"The girl's father. He was calling. He wants her back."

TWO DOORS DOWN the hall, inside a bathroom, Amena heard the words and stood up. She had no father. He had been killed. There was only one man who could claim that title, and she was ashamed she'd run from him.

Pike was looking for her. Hunting her, like he had in the past.

She sagged against the door, the relief flooding through her. She had seen what he would do for someone he loved, and she dared to believe he might love her.

She curled into a ball, pushing her ear against the door, listening.

She heard Beth get slapped again, and then heard her wail that she had the information on the john she had been with. The man had bragged to her in Norfolk about being some sort of bigwig in the U.S. Navy, and now she'd found out why he was here in Charleston. Trying to stave off more pain, Beth whimpered that she had something that could provide leverage.

The Enforcer smacked her again, shouting, "What good does that do us?"

Beth told them what she knew about the man's occupation and Slaven said, "That does us a lot of good. I have some friends who would love to have information he can provide. This will be worth more than all of the work we do here. I promise."

"How?"

"You remember those Russian guys we helped find a place to stay in the United States? The recruiters for Wagner that wanted us to join? They're tied into the Russian government and they'll pay for whatever this man can give, I promise."

"How do we get it?"

"We have his information, and the fact that he paid for Beth. It's enough, trust me. He works for the U.S. government. He won't want that little story out. I've seen those Russians do the same thing. I'll text him, telling him his life is over if he doesn't produce. It might take a day or two of convincing, but he'll eventually give in. I've seen it before, in Europe."

"That's a risky play. This guy is an unknown, and we might need more men to control it. I say fuck him and deal with the problem here. The guy chasing the little bitch in the bathroom."

Amena cringed at being singled out, then heard, "Wait, wait. I agree with that, but this is worth serious money. We *do* need more men. What about Branko?

He's in Myrtle Beach, and he's got a crew of four. You know him, right? Can you get him down here?"

"Yeah. I can get him. He can be here in an hour or two, but why?"

"Because we're going to make a big payday. Make the call."

Amena went back to the door, this time putting her eye to the old keyhole, seeing Radovan talking to Slaven, Beth on the floor between them on her knees, her head down.

Radovan slapped her face, and the one they called the doctor came forward holding a laptop, saying, "Wait, wait, don't bruise her. She has another date."

Radovan stood with his fists balled, Beth cowering in front of him. Slaven took the laptop and said, "What do you mean?"

The doctor said, "She's got another date from the webpage. We aren't at a total loss."

Radovan sneered and said, "Screw that. We need to find out who the man was that called. The one who broke up the first date. The one who owns the girl. He's a threat."

Slaven said, "You're right, of course. Call the men at Myrtle Beach. It's another reason to get them here."

Radovan nodded, considering, then walked away, his phone to his ear. Amena watched Slaven study the laptop, saying, "Someone else has asked for a date?"

The doctor said, "Yeah. I don't know how, but she's been requested."

Slaven looked at the screen and said, "I thought she was booked with this other asshole? For the entire night? How did that happen?"

"I don't know, but it works in our favor. The guy deleted his profile and she became available again. The new guy will get us at least half the money we lost with the whale."

Slaven said, "He deleted his profile? That's not good. We need to use it for leverage. Can you bring it back?"

"I get screenshots of all transactions and track their IP addresses, MAC addresses, everything. I have his. He's done."

Slaven nodded, then looked at the request. Radovan came back into the hallway and said, "They're on the way. What's up?"

"Nothing. It just looks like we're going to make up for Beth's fuckup tonight."

Radovan took the computer, studied it, then said, "Doc, what's the MAC address used to make the original date?"

Doc took the computer, dug around in the hard drive, then brought up the old account. Radovan looked at it, then said, "It's the man who called. That's who it is. He tracked your 'whale' down and now he's hunting."

Her eye pressed to the keyhole, Amena saw Slaven take the computer back, saying, "Oh, come on. That's bullshit."

Radovan said, "Look at the MAC addresses. They're the same. This account was made on the same computer as the old account. He's trying to find the girl, and he found the one connection to this bitch here."

Slaven scrolled down the computer screen and saw what Radovan said was true. Without conviction, he said, "That still doesn't prove it's the guy that called."

Radovan snarled, "It's close enough to worry about." He pointed at Beth, and she cowered. He slapped her into the wall and said, "Who is this guy?"

She said, "I don't know. I honestly don't know." And then, because she wanted to stop the pain, but hating herself all the same, she pointed at the bathroom and said, "But the girl does."

Amena backed away from the keyhole and locked the door, waiting on the inevitable. She heard the footsteps coming down the hall, then the Enforcer outside of the door. He jerked the handle, cursed, and said, "Open this."

She retreated inside the bathroom, pulling off the rod for the towel rack, the only weapon she had. She waited, hearing nothing. Nobody kicked in the door. Nobody said a word.

Then she heard Slaven, the one man who'd been kind to her. He said, "Open the door, please."

She did nothing.

He waited a beat, and then said, "Open the door, or you're going to cause someone you like to be harmed."

She sidled to the keyhole and saw him holding Beth's head in both hands. He squeezed her skull, causing Beth to let out a keening wail.

She shouted, "Stop it! If I open the door, you're going to hurt me, too."

Slaven said, "No, I'm not, but I will hurt Beth. It's your choice." She then saw him tie his hand into Beth's hair and jerk, extracting a scream.

He said, "You are causing this. Only you can make it stop."

Amena knew he was lying. Knew he was evil, and because of it, she understood that opening the door was a bad decision, but she couldn't be responsible for the torture Slaven was inflicting.

But she also knew something these men did not. She had someone looking for her. Someone who could bring an inferno to save her. Unlike Beth's parents, Jennifer and Pike weren't impotent.

They were a wrecking machine.

The one unknown was whether they truly cared about her, but they were the closest people she had to family left on this earth. Deep in her heart, though, she was still unsure of their love, and knew she was placing everything in their hands. But she had no other choice.

She closed her eyes, sent a prayer out into the universe, and unlocked the door.

Chapter 9

JENNIFER WATCHED THE Hyundai leave the garage and got her first eyes on the target. A balding man of about fifty with a full beard. She let him pass, checked that the tracker was transmitting, and called Pike.

"Target's out of the nest and moving up East Bay, headed to the Ravenel Bridge."

"Roger all. I'm a block over near the fountain. No joy on Amena."

"You want me to engage?"

"Not yet. Keep eyes on the beacon. He's got three choices here: Break off East Bay into the city, take the Ravenel to Mount Pleasant, or keep going north toward North Charleston."

She said, "Or get on Interstate 26."

"He can't get to 26 from East Bay."

"I know, but it's a choice. All he has to do is cut over to Meeting Street."

Pike said, "Good point. So four choices. Keep eyes on and commit when he does. The trigger will be the Ravenel Bridge. I'm circling around to East Bay."

"He just hung a left. He's on Meeting Street now."

"Okay, okay. Let it play out."

"He just passed the bridge. Still headed north."

"Start moving that way. I'll let you lead."

She put her car in gear and began driving, wondering how smart this half-baked surveillance effort was. She wanted to find Amena more than life itself, and she knew Pike felt the same, but wondered if he wasn't projecting a solution that would take them away from a more productive thread. She also questioned how Pike had found this guy.

But she knew the answer. He'd leveraged the Taskforce, just as she'd asked. She understood it was patently illegal, and not something she should sanction, but she did. She'd learned a little bit about the evil in the world since colliding with Pike Logan, and where she once would have balked at his walking on the edge, she no longer did, sometimes even encouraging him to lean over. It looked like he had here.

She raced up Meeting Street, seeing on her tablet that the car had entered the interstate, still headed north. She gave Pike the information, and then entered the freeway herself, the car five miles ahead.

Twenty minutes later he was off the interstate and the beacon was stationary. She exited, following the beacon track, and found herself at a Staybridge Inn, north of Charleston, near Goose Creek.

He's at another hotel?

She pulled into the parking lot, noticing that this hotel was not nearly as fancy as the one downtown. A place for longer-term stays, it was utilitarian, with what looked like military men and women coming and going, in an area that was full of strip malls and used car lots.

She said, "Pike, this is Koko, he's stopped, but it wasn't at a house. It's another hotel. The Staybridge Inn on Ashley Phosphate."

Pike said, "Hotel? Shit, that's no help. We don't know the room."

She felt his frustration, and was about to respond when he said, "Hold what you got. I'm going back to the Taskforce."

"Who are you talking to?"

"Creed. He won't like it, though."

"Hang on. Don't burn that bridge. Let me do a little social engineering. I'll find his room the old-fashioned way."

"How's that?"

She opened the door and said, "I'll show the desk clerk some cleavage."

She heard Pike splutter and jogged to the side of the building, looking for an entrance. She said, "Calm down, Neanderthal. I'm just kidding. I have an idea. If it doesn't pan out, then pull the trigger on Creed."

He said, "What? What idea? I'm twenty minutes out."

She said, "Trust me. We'll know by the time you get here. How long was the car rental for?"

She had a plan of attack, and because of it she didn't want to walk straight into the lobby, preferring to enter where it looked to the desk clerk like she was already inside. She found a side door with a key-card access panel. She pulled the handle, hoping it was only in use at night.

It was.

She skirted down the hallway, looked left, and saw Lannister McBride waiting on the elevator holding a Coke and a microwave dinner from the hotel store. She ducked back inside the hallway, waiting.

She heard the bell for the elevator, paused another second, then turned the corner, marching into the lobby. She went straight to the front desk, seeing a clean-shaven black man behind the counter.

He said, "Can I help you?"

"Yeah, you can. I'm a little embarrassed. I just left my room, but without my key. I've locked myself out."

He smiled and said, "No problem. Room number?"

"Lannister McBride."

He tapped it into the computer and said, "Room 404?"

"That's it."

He frowned at the screen and said, "Lannister McBride? He's here by himself."

Jennifer turned on the wattage of her smile and said, "He is. I'm his wife. He got here two weeks ago, and he's here for another three. I'm just visiting for the weekend."

The man behind the counter returned the smile and said, "Sounds like he's working at the navy base."

He ran a new key card through the access control, then said, "Charleston's a good place to visit, I'll give you that."

He held out the key and she took it, then saw him squint his eyes at the screen again, saying, "Hey, he just came through here. I sold him a microwave dinner."

She turned and said, "Yeah, trust me, he's not eating that when I'm here. We're going out."

He laughed and said, "You go, girl."

She reached the elevator feeling the sweat on her neck at her subterfuge.

She pressed the button and said on the net, "I have him. I'll call when complete."

Pike said, "I'm almost at the parking lot. Turn on your speaker phone. I want to hear what's happening."

She dug her phone out of her purse, activated the speaker function, then said, "Why is that? You don't trust me?"

"No, no. It's not that. I just want to be able to react if I need to. Before you can call."

She entered the elevator and said, "Don't come up here unless it's an emergency. You sent me in here for reason. Don't screw it up."

The elevator stopped on the fourth floor and she heard, "I know, I know. Just find that girl."

Room 404 was two rooms off of the elevator foyer. She approached the door and said, "About to make contact. Can't talk anymore."

"Roger all. In the parking lot."

She hesitated, then knocked. She heard a shuffling and could feel the man behind the door looking at her through the peephole.

She heard, "What do you want?"

"Mr. McBride, I'm with the hotel staff and we have an indication your carbon monoxide monitor is out. I just need to come in and check it."

"Do it later. After I've gone to work tomorrow. I have to go to bed."

"Sir, I must insist."

"Get out of here."

She heard the shuffling go away and pulled out her key card, sliding it into the slot. The light went green and she pushed the door open, entering a small suite complete with a kitchenette, sofa, and a king-sized bed to the left. She turned and saw Lannister with his mouth open at her entrance. He was bigger than he looked in the car, probably topping out at six-foot-two, with a healthy gut.

He said, "What the fuck are you doing? I said come back tomorrow, when I'm at work."

She held up her hands and said, "Lannister, my name is Jennifer Cahill, and I'm here trying to find the

woman you were with earlier. I don't care who you are, and I don't care who she is, but she could be a link to a missing girl."

His eyes went wide and he said, "Who the fuck are you people? I don't know about any girl. Get out of my room!"

"We know you were with a woman today. That's who we want to talk to, not you. Just tell us how to find her."

On her earpiece she heard Pike say, "What's the room number? Get me up there."

She imagined Pike was frothing at the mouth, but ignored him, focusing on Lannister, knowing that if Pike entered the room, this guy would more than likely go to the hospital. Violence wouldn't solve this problem.

Lannister advanced on her with his fists balled, the veins on his neck jutting out. Through clenched teeth he snarled, "Get out of my room, now."

He entered into her personal space and, unbidden, she reacted, snapping two palm strikes to his nose, popping his head back like he'd been hit with a bat, then spearing his groin with a knee.

She bounced back, fists raised, and he dropped to the floor, moaning. He writhed around for a second clutching his privates, then moaned, "Jesus Christ! I wasn't going to attack you."

He spit out a wad of vomit, and she thought, *Oops.*

He continued flopping like a worm on hot pavement and she said, "I'm sorry. I thought you were going to hit me."

From Pike, she heard, "I'm in the lobby What the fuck is going on? What room?"

She said, "It's a 1202 emergency. I'm good."

She heard him laugh, calming down. He said, "Let me know. I'm here."

A month before, they'd both watched a documentary about the Apollo 11 moon landing, and had marveled at how calm Neil Armstrong and his crew were on the mission. Ten seconds before the lunar lander was supposed to touch down on the moon, the computer had started bleating out something called a "1202 emergency," which was an overload of the computers designed to facilitate his landing and an immediate abort. Armstrong had chosen to ignore the warning and had landed anyway. It turned out, the computer was bleating for no reason, and it hadn't been an emergency.

She used the term because she knew it would turn off Pike's Neanderthal instincts. If she could come up with that in the spur of the moment, he would know she was good.

Lannister's panting slowed and he wiped the vomit from the corner of his mouth, then the blood off his nose, but didn't get off the floor. He said, "What do you want?"

"The girl. We want to talk to the girl."

He said, "I didn't know she was a prostitute. It was supposed to be a date."

Yeah, right.

"That's fine. We don't care about what you did. We want to talk to her. How do we find her?"

He said, "Can I go to my computer?"

She said, "Yeah, sure. Just do it slowly."

He went to it, pulled up a website, and she saw a bunch of half-naked women all advertising services here in Charleston. He pulled up one of the ads and she recognized the woman from the fountain.

Ten minutes later, she left the room, calling Pike. "I have her."

"Where? Where is she?"

"I don't know right now, but you've got a date with her in an hour."

Chapter 10

LANNISTER MCBRIDE SAT on his bed holding his head in his hands, wondering how much this was going to affect his life. Wishing he hadn't been so stupid.

He'd never had trouble before, with each woman he'd slept with seeming to like his overt attempt to turn the contract arrangement into a full-on date night. In his heart, he knew it was a chimera, but it helped him sleep at night. He wasn't hiring whores. He was just going on a date. Or so he told himself.

And now *this* had happened.

He had no earthly idea what the story was with the girl the woman was seeking, but knew it couldn't be good. First, the man had called at his private love nest, and now the woman had showed up here. That wasn't because they were lucky. It was because they *knew*. They had somehow found him based on his contact with

Beth, and Beth had some contact with the girl. They weren't fucking around, and he feared for his future.

He was the quality control for some of the most classified instructions of the United States Navy. He was entrusted with the deepest secrets the navy held. Being exposed as sleeping with a whore at every port—because he'd slept with Beth in Norfolk once before—would end his life. He would lose his security clearance, and with it his ability to make a living.

And then he thought of his wife. She would leave him for sure, taking their kids with her. He'd been caught sleeping around twice before, and she'd left him on the last one. It had taken months to rebuild the relationship, and if this got out, she would leave for sure, ripping apart his navy pension and crushing him into oblivion. Because there was no doubt she would win.

He put his head in his hands and sobbed, then, after a moment, he began to rationalize. Both the man on the phone and the woman had said they didn't care what he was doing. They only wanted to talk to the girl. He'd deleted his profile on the sex site and was due to go to work tomorrow like a normal day. Maybe it would just go away. He'd given them what they wanted.

He sniffled, thinking that the worst may have already happened. He wasn't the target, his date was. Let them do their work. It didn't involve him.

But it did. He didn't realize his world was about to get exponentially worse until his phone pinged with a text.

He pulled it up and saw:

Lannister McBride, you had a date with a female today, and we need to talk. We have pictures. I will call. You will answer.

He felt his heart about to explode as it pumped adrenaline into his system. He sat catatonic for a moment, and then his cell phone rang.

He watched the buzzing phone, not wanting to touch it. Finally, he swiped right and brought the cell to his ear.

"Hello?"

"Hello, Lannister McBride. My name is Slaven, and you ditched a girl of mine tonight. I need payment."

Trying to bluster, Lannister said, "Hey, wait a minute, we didn't do anything. She said she had to leave."

"No, she didn't."

Lannister paused, then said, "Okay, okay, I'll pay. I'll pay for the entire night."

"Thank you for being amenable. That is good news. I hate to fight for payment."

Sweating, Lannister said, "How do we do this? How much do you want?"

"Well, there we're in a bit of a sticky wicket. I don't want money. I want what you can get from the nuclear propulsion school."

Shocked, Lannister said nothing. Slaven said, "You still there?"

"I . . . I don't know what you're talking about."

"Yes, you do. You shouldn't have had so much pillow talk with my girl in Norfolk. She told me why you're here. You're a contractor for the nuclear school, responsible for the safety of the two test submarines they use for training. You have access to a lot of valuable data. I'm not asking for anything super-secret. Just the maintenance records."

Lannister knew that those records were in fact top secret and could expose vulnerabilities in the United States nuclear fleet. He said, "I can't do that."

"Yes, you can. In fact, you're the only one who can. And you can learn a lesson about bragging to a whore."

Instead of reverting to a sense of patriotism, Lannister deflected to pragmatism. "No, I mean I can't do it because it's all locked down. I can't get access without them knowing I did so. I can't remove anything."

Slaven said, "Well, unless you want your world destroyed, you'll find a way. Do you understand?"

Lannister stalled for a moment, then said, "I can't do that. Don't ask me for that. I can pay. I'll pay you for the girl."

His voice soothing over the phone, Slaven said, "It's too late for that now. Pay attention to what I'm saying. Get me something from the maintenance records. Do as I ask, or I'll crush your life with the information I have."

Lannister dropped the phone like it was molten rock, then began pulling out his thinning hair and rocking back and forth. He heard something from the speaker and ignored it. He heard it again, and picked the phone back up, hearing, ". . . you there?"

"I'm here."

"Good. Listen, this is just a one-time thing. For a one-time payment. You do this and I'll go my way, and you go yours. Understand?"

Lannister heard the words and began to rationalize again, seeing a way out of his predicament. It would be damn near impossible to get the data this man wanted, as all of the computers were tracked by login and extraction, but it might be able to be done. Just last year there had been a teacher/student scandal at this very post where the instructors were selling the tests to the students for a passing grade—and those tests were under the same top secret classification he was going to have to penetrate. If they could do it, more than likely, so could he.

He said, "You'll never mention the girl? You'll leave me alone?"

"Yes. I promise."

Lannister squeezed his eyes shut, thinking. Begging for a solution. He heard, "Are we agreed?"

And he committed, like so many traitors before him. "Yes. Just this one time."

"Good. I'll text you the link-up information. Expect it to be tomorrow."

"Wait! That can't happen. I have to go to work tomorrow, and it's going to take me some time to figure out how to extract the data. I can't do it in a day."

He heard a breath, then, "Okay, two days. Look for a text from the same number you got before."

The phone went dead and Lannister dropped his hand, then sagged back onto his bed, wondering how his life had turned into a quagmire.

EXILE EVE 65

Chapter 11

INSIDE THE CHEAP motel cottage on Folly Beach that Slaven had found, Beth sat on the squeaky bed, fidgeting enough to make noise, wondering who would enter through the door. Would it be another john? Or Amena's father?

She prayed it was just another customer, because if it was the father, things were going to get exponentially more complicated. She could live with sleeping with a stranger—that had been beaten into her—but she didn't know what she would do if she were offered the chance to escape.

If it was the father, he was searching for his daughter, and in that search, she could be free. He wouldn't want to sleep with her, and she could use that to escape.

The second that thought entered her head, she banished it. Her life wasn't worth ending Tess and Misty's lives. Not to mention the girl. If she ran, Slaven had said he would kill them all.

She put her head in her hands, for the first time begging that the man who entered simply wanted to fuck her. If not, she was supposed to take him to Slaven and the girl. Where she was sure the innocent man would be killed.

She heard a knock on the door and tensed. It happened again, and she advanced, opening it to find a man who looked like he killed for a living. Over six feet tall, without an ounce of fat, he had ice blue eyes and a scar that tracked a path down through his cheek. She stumbled back and he said, "Hey, my name's Pike. Are you Beth?"

She nodded, feeling relief. *He's not the father.* Then she felt apprehension, thinking, *He's going to be rough with me.*

She held open the door, subservient, and he said, "So, how does this work?"

"Well, you tell me what you like, and I tell you a price, but I have to say, I'm not into BDSM or any rough play."

He entered and shut the door, then locked it, amping up her fear. He turned to her and said, "I won't be rough, I promise. In fact, I'll pay you for the entire night without even sleeping with you."

And she saw a flicker of kindness in his eyes. Like he was a priest or something.

What is going on?

She said, "What does that mean? I'm not going to be using toys for you to watch. That's not what I do. You saw the webpage. Straight sex. *That's* what I do."

He said, "Can we sit down?"

She nodded, and he pulled a chair away from a chipped plastic table in the makeshift kitchen, causing a roach to scurry away. He sat down and said, "This is a far cry from the French Quarter Inn."

The words sank in, and she made the connection. "You're the father."

She saw his face register surprise, and he said, "Yeah, wait, what? How do you know that?"

She wanted to scream, *They have her, and they're going to kill you. Get out of here!*

Instead, she began her rehearsed speech, "The girl is with my friends, and she doesn't want anything to do with you. She wants to be free."

"What the hell are you talking about? Where is she?"

"She's with my friends. She wants to leave you, and she will. She said you're an asshole and she wants a different life. That's all."

Pike sat up in his chair, and she felt the full potential of his violence. He snarled, "Where. Is. She?"

She recoiled, wanting to tell him everything. Wanted to let it all out, about the exit fee, the deaths she'd seen, the wanton cruelty, but she remembered Tess and Misty. There was no way this man could save them, even if he was as skilled as he looked.

She said, "She's safe. In fact, if you want to talk to her, we'll go meet her. She can tell you herself."

He said, "Okay, I'd like that. Where?"

She said, "Hang on," then dialed a cell phone, talking to Slaven. When she was done, she said, "It's just down the street. A restaurant called Rita's. But be careful. The people we are with may hurt you if you make a scene."

He stood up, towering over her, and said, "I fucking doubt that."

She saw his eyes flash, and instead of fear, she felt his pain.

She wished her own parents were like him, and felt a debilitating terror that the girl would leave and she would be forced to stay. Why hadn't her own father done what this man was doing? Was she not worth it? What made this girl different?

The man put his hand on her arm, not in a violent way, and said, "Take me to them. Let's have a talk."

She looked up at him and saw a force unlike that of the men who held her. The violence was there, but not the cruelty. As instructed, thinking of Tess and Misty, she made one last attempt, saying, "Don't do anything stupid. She doesn't want to be with you. Let it go."

He said, "Yeah, I'll do that after I see her. But I'm pretty sure your idea of letting it go isn't the same as mine."

And for the first time, she dared to believe that she might be free.

Chapter 12

AMENA WAS SHOVED into the car between two other burly men. One was from the new crew out of Myrtle Beach, but the other was the Enforcer. Slaven put the car into drive, saying, "Remember what we talked about, little girl. You get this man to quit. You are a refugee, and if you mess with me, I'll not only get you sent back to Syria, I'll kill Beth, Tess, and Misty. Okay?"

Scared out of her mind, Amena nodded.

A lot had happened in the last three hours, to the point where she wished she *were* back in Syria. At least in the time before the war had started. Then, she would have her family. Her father, brother, and mother. But they were all dead, and now she was going to face the same for coming to the one land she believed would allow her to live.

When she'd unlocked the bathroom door, the Enforcer had slammed it open, then grabbed her by her hair, flinging her into the hallway next to Beth. Beth had mouthed, *I'm sorry*, and then Slaven had slapped Amena hard in the face, knocking her to the ground.

He'd asked her about her "father," and she'd lied, trying to protect her new family. Trying to protect Pike and Jennifer. He'd become incensed, screaming, "Nobody works that hard to find someone they don't care about. Who is he?"

And she'd given him her story. All of it, to include that she was an illegal refugee in the land of the free and the brave, only twisting the story to make it seem like Pike and Jennifer were some sort of international coyotes who were smuggling in people like her for pay—and that Pike hadn't been paid yet.

Slaven had said, "So this is all about money? Your real father promised payment and this guy doesn't have it yet?"

She'd nodded, saying, "He died before he could provide it, and I don't have it."

Slaven smiled, saying, "This is going to be easy. You just tell him you're glad to be away from him. Can you do that?"

Slaven had told her what the punishment would be if she tried to go back to her "daddy"—apparently a slang term that these men used with their slaves. If she said anything wrong at the meeting, they would kill the women, and she couldn't be responsible for that. In her mind, she thought she'd find a way to escape, just like she had in Europe, but deep inside she knew these men who held her wouldn't let that happen. They had Beth, Misty, and that girl Tess—tied to a bed with Frankenstein stitches. If they couldn't escape, how could she?

She'd nodded again, and he'd said, "Do what I ask and you'll be away from that asshole. You'll be with friends. Understand?"

Without conviction, she said, "Yes."

He grabbed her by her hair and said, "Do you *understand*? You aren't his anymore. You're mine."

She said, "Yes, daddy. Yes."

He'd liked the answer, and then they'd waited, sitting on a couch in the living room. Thirty minutes later, four men had entered, all looking like the Enforcer. Hard men with tattoos and scars. Slaven had embraced them, and then spoken in a language she didn't understand, but she could see where this was headed, and it wasn't good.

She'd felt the tears well up and was ashamed at her weakness. She had brought this on herself by running from Pike, and she deserved what came. She couldn't do anything tonight, because that would put the women in the house in jeopardy, along with Pike and Jennifer. She would have to wait, but in her heart she was sure that in the waiting, she would lose. It tore at her, not the least because she wasn't even sure how much Pike truly cared for her. Even if she tried to warn him, he might just toss her aside like all the other men she'd met on her odyssey from Syria. Deep in her heart, she didn't believe that—after all, it was Pike who'd saved her life in Switzerland and brought her to America—but she was afraid to put her trust to the test.

The only two men she'd ever trusted were her father and her brother. And they were both dead.

Eventually, Beth had left the house, going to some hole-in-the-wall motel down the street to meet her john, and Amena was torn between wanting it to be Pike and not wanting it to be Pike.

And then the call had come from Beth. It was Pike.

She'd been crammed into a car between the two rough men, then driven about two miles to an indoor-outdoor cafe called Rita's. She was hustled inside and saw the place was jam-packed, with a live band, the cacophony of noise assaulting her ears. She was led to a back booth in the corner of the restaurant, all by itself at the edge of the crowd.

She was shoved into a seat and found herself facing Pike Logan and Beth. She wanted to smile, but knew that would kill the girls. She maintained her surly appearance, and saw his confusion.

He said, "Hey, doodlebug. Good to see you."

Slaven said, "Get out of the booth."

Pike said, "What for?"

"Because I said so. Beth, you come over here."

Pike exited, and one of the rough men slid in. Slaven said, "Have a seat." Pike did so, and the Enforcer slid in to his right. Beth took a seat next to Slaven.

Pike said, "Hey, I don't want any trouble. I just want my girl back."

Slaven said, "She doesn't want to go back with you. She has some new friends now, and we aren't paying your freight. Understand?"

Amena saw Pike's eyes narrow and knew this was going to be an endgame. She couldn't let that happen. Couldn't be responsible for his death.

"I don't want to be with you anymore," she said to Pike. "I want to be with them, and if you try to prevent that, they'll stop you. I don't have the money you're owed, but I'm done with you." She could barely look at him.

In her heart, she wanted Pike to destroy everyone in the booth, but she knew he couldn't do that. He was good, but not that good.

Slaven said, "So, you heard her. Time to go. You wanted a payment, but that isn't coming. You leave here now, and you'll get to go on your own two feet. You choose to fight for your little bit of money and you'll exit in a body bag."

Pike bored into Amena's eyes and said, "I have no idea what you're talking about. I want my little doodlebug."

Amena felt Slaven's hand on her knee, squeezing like a vise. She wanted to tell Pike *so bad* what was happening. Wanted to tell him what was at stake. Wanted to have him help her, but in so doing, she would put his life in jeopardy.

In that moment, she realized she loved him.

Loved him and Jennifer like her own flesh and blood, and because of it she was forced to sacrifice to spare them. She wanted the love returned, but she knew that wasn't going to happen. Her flesh and blood had died in Syria.

Slaven squeezed her knee again and said, "Tell him to leave. Let him know it's you that wants this."

She felt the tears well up in her eyes, wanting to say the words, and couldn't. She couldn't bring herself to send her body to hell. She looked at Pike, wanting to find some reciprocal love, and saw nothing but a brooding man. She said, "I . . . I . . ."

Slaven squeezed her knee again, and she desperately sought a way to let Pike know that she was in danger. Something Slaven wouldn't understand, but Pike would. She found it, and took a leap off of a cliff, praying she was right about his affection. Begging to believe.

Amena locked eyes with Pike and said, "Winter is here."

She saw relief flood across Pike's face, his expression visibly relaxing, like he'd confirmed something. It was only a split-second reaction, and then she saw his face harden, his eyes boring into hers with the truth she had been seeking. He nodded. Nobody else seemed to notice, but she did, and she finally understood why.

He loved her.

Slaven clamped his hand on her leg until she yelped, saying, "What the fuck does that mean? Winter what?"

She kept her eyes on Pike, and she saw a hint of a smile. She fought to contain her own. She knew he would be forced to leave her here with the men, but he would come for her. He was completely overmatched in the booth, but he wouldn't be the next time. It was the best she could do.

Slaven said again, "What do you mean about winter?"

Pike ignored him. Speaking to her alone, he said, "Yes, winter is here. Because *I am winter.*"

Faster than she could follow, he whipped his elbow to the left, crushing the nose of the man next to him and bouncing his head off the back of the booth. The man fell forward onto the table, unconscious, and Pike hammered the back of his neck like he was breaking the vertebrae of a rabbit for slaughter. There was a snap like a broken twig, and the man sagged.

The Enforcer sprang back in surprise, and Pike jammed the first two fingers of his right hand into his eye orbits, causing him to scream and thrash. Pike drove his head back until his throat was clear, then backhanded a strike into the cartilage of his neck, smashing it. The Enforcer's eyes bulged out and he put his hands to his throat, coughing and spluttering, his face turning red. Pike slammed his head into the table hard enough to knock him out, and the body sank into the corner of the booth, his life slowly extinguished by the lack of oxygen from his shattered windpipe.

The entire action took less than five seconds. Two dead men, both lying next to Pike. Slaven was incredulous. He jumped up, pulling a small pocket pistol from his waist, and Amena grabbed his wrist, latching onto it with her mouth, biting as hard as she could.

Slaven screamed, and Pike stood up, throwing a right cross with his whole body behind it, snapping his hips and cracking Slaven in the temple with a blow that could have felled a bull. He collapsed on the table, unconscious.

Nobody said anything. Amena looked at Pike in awe, her eyes wide open, trying to get her mind around what he'd just accomplished. Beth looked sick to her stomach, rocking back and forth in the booth.

Pike glanced left and right and nothing happened, the music so loud and the crowd so packed that nobody had even noticed the action.

He returned to Amena and said, "Doodlebug, you want to go home?"

She stood up on the bench and then launched herself across the table, cinching her legs around him and saying, "I'm sorry. I'm so sorry."

He wrapped her in his arms and said, "Nothing to be sorry for."

She leaned back and said, "They said my father was coming. . . ."

"Yeah, so?"

"Why would they say that?"

She saw Pike duck his head a little bit, then rise back up. "I can't be your father. But I can be the next best thing."

She squeezed him like she never wanted to let go, then said, "Where's Jennifer? Why isn't she here?"

Pike laughed and said, "She's outside. Waiting on you."

"What's that mean?"

"Don't tell her I told you this, but if I'd have been killed in here, she was going to kill everyone exiting to free you."

And the depth of his commitment came home. She said, "So you knew I was lying?"

"Of course I did."

For the first time since the loss of her family, she felt whole. Amena said, "Where is she?"

"Right outside, in the parking lot out back. Go chase her down, but don't do anything scary, because she might shoot you."

Amena grinned, and then said, "There are more that need saving. We can't just drive away. There's a girl with a surgical thing going on and another one named Misty."

She looked at Beth and said, "And there's Beth. They all need to be saved."

Pike said, "Go find Jennifer. Take Beth with you. Let me solve the rest."

Amena squeezed him with her arms for a second, then dropped down.

She took Beth's hand and said, "That's *my* daddy," then raced into the crowd, dragging Beth behind her.

Chapter 13

I LET AMENA scamper away, then glanced around the room, the music bouncing off the walls, the floor packed with drunk beach patrons. Nobody was paying any attention to our table. Luckily, the idiot I'd knocked out had demanded we be in the corner, which helped, but there was only so long I wanted to remain with two dead guys and an unconscious one. Sooner or later, a waitress would ask if we wanted anything, and I was pretty sure the folks at the table wouldn't answer.

I searched the two men I'd killed, retrieving their wallets and cell phones and finding two handguns; one a CZ 75 and another a beat-up Browning Hi-Power. I shoved both into my waistband, then scrambled around for the pocket pistol Slaven had brandished.

I found it under the table, stood up, and saw a waitress making her way through the crowd. That would not work.

I shouldered my way past the cordon of people and touched her elbow, saying, "Hey, I'm going to cover that back table. We're done with the drinks, but we'd like to stay a little bit longer."

I gave her four twenties and said, "Keep the rest."

She smiled and I walked back to the table, wondering how I was going to get the man known as Slaven to wake up. I decided on the expedient route, picking up my glass of water and dumping it on his face.

He spluttered, and I saw his eyes flutter open. I jammed the Browning Hi-Power into his ribs and said, "Stand up slowly and you might live. Unlike your friends."

I saw his eyes focus on the two dead men across the table, and then he sluggishly rose. I said, "Keep your hands to the front. Lace them together."

He did so, and I said, "We're going out the back, right now. If you try anything, I'll put a bullet in your heart and simply run away. Do not underestimate my desire to kill you."

He nodded, and we pushed our way through the crowd, exiting onto the back patio. I prodded him to a six-foot wooden fence at the back of the patio, a single gate in the middle for trash removal. I said, "Open it."

He did so, and we spilled out into a gravel parking lot jammed with vehicles, throngs of people coming and going. I called Jennifer and said, "We're out. Where are you?"

"I see you. Back row. Keep coming."

I did and found her with Amena and Beth, Amena bouncing up and down on her toes and Beth looking sick to her stomach.

Jennifer said, "What happened in there?"

"Nothing. Just solved a problem."

She gave me her disapproving teacher glare and said, "Amena said you slaughtered two men."

I pushed Slaven forward and said, "It could have been three. Ask Beth if they deserved it."

Jennifer grinned and said, "Okay, okay, Amena told me that as well. What now?"

Honestly, I wasn't sure. I had Amena back safe and sound, and could just dump Slaven at the nearest police station, implicating him in everything he'd been doing, but Amena had said that others were at risk, here, on Folly Beach. I decided to explore a little bit.

I said, "Take Amena to the motel room."

Jennifer had been outside of the motel cottage when I'd met Beth, and had followed us to the restaurant, so she knew where to go.

"What are you going to do?"

"Meet you there. Beth, you're going to drive my Jeep. Can you work a standard transmission?"

She nodded; then, like a robot, she said, "I have to go. Get back. I don't want to be a part of this."

I realized how much the trauma of her captivity had penetrated her psyche. She was still worried about the men, refusing to believe she had been saved.

I said, "Beth, you're not going back there, ever. You're free. Trust me."

Out of nowhere, Slaven said, "You're still mine. Remember that. Remember what will happen if you help."

She cowered and said, "I'm sorry, daddy. I didn't do this. I did what you asked. It's not my fault."

Her reaction to his words infuriated me. I cocked my fist and slammed it into Slaven's kidney, bringing him to his knees. I jerked his head up by the hair, looked into his eyes, and said, "You're trying my patience. If you say one more word, I'll fucking cut your throat."

He opened his mouth, and I raised a finger, saying, "Think. If you utter a sound, you are dead."

He closed his mouth and I turned to Beth, saying, "Come on. You drive. I'll be in the backseat with him. He can't hurt you anymore. Nobody can."

She nodded, struggling to believe. I turned to Jennifer and said, "See you at the motel."

She took Amena's hand and kissed me on the cheek, whispering, "Don't kill him on the drive."

I smiled and said, "I won't. I need him."

Ten minutes later, we were at the shithole motel, me pushing Slaven forward while Beth trailed behind. We reached the cottage where I'd met her, and I said, "Beth, knock on the door."

She did, and Jennifer opened it. I pushed Slaven forward saying, "Find me something to restrain this guy and gag him."

In short order I had him on the floor of the disgusting bathroom, the roaches crawling on him, his legs bent and tied to his arms behind his back, his mouth gagged and a rag cinched over his eyes.

I leaned down and thumped his head into the floorboard, saying, "You try anything at all, and you're dead. If you so much as twitch, I'll kill you."

I stood up and said, "Amena, Jennifer and I are going to talk to Beth. I want you to stay here and watch him. If he makes any move—and I mean *any* move—come out and tell me."

She nodded like it was a game, all smiles. She said, "Can I kick him first? Before I come out?"

I said, "By all means. But aim for his nuts when you do."

Jennifer slapped my shoulder and said, "No. No, Amena, you can't kick him. Just come out and tell us."

We exited and Jennifer hissed, "What are you trying to teach her?"

I smiled and said, "That guy deserves a kick to the nuts."

She said, "He certainly does, but you don't tell Amena that."

We entered the bedroom and found Beth sitting on the mattress, fidgeting and working her hands through her hair and clutching her shirt.

Jennifer sat next to her and said, "So, what's your story?"

"What are you going to do to me? What do you want? I can sleep with you if that's what you would like, but you have to let me go back after. I don't even want any money."

I sat on her other side and put my hand on her shoulder, causing her to jump. I said, "Hey, hey, we don't want anything from you. We wanted to find Amena. That's all. You can leave if you want, but apparently we've found something more than we bargained for."

She looked at me with an earnestness that penetrated my soul, wanting to believe our good intentions, but not wanting to have her trust shattered yet again. She said, "I can leave here now? Walk right out that door?"

"Yes. I promise."

Tears formed in her eyes and she said, "I've heard 'I promise' before, from Slaven. Right after that, I never saw my family again."

I realized she had been trained to submit. Trained by punishment. I looked at Jennifer and saw her beginning to tear up. She gently brushed Beth's cheek and said, "When we say it, we mean it. Now what was Amena talking about with other girls? What's an 'exit fee'?"

Beth fought back a whimper, looked at Jennifer, then at me, and said, "These men are evil. They will kill all of us if they get the chance. You don't know them like I do."

I leaned in and said, "I *want* to know them. Tell me. What's the exit fee?"

She started crying and said, "They capture girls like me, and then force us to have sex. If you want to leave, you have to pay an exit fee. I couldn't do it."

"What's the fee?"

She looked at me, wiped her nose, and said, "A kidney."

The word hung in the air, and neither Jennifer nor I could believe it. Incredulous, I said, "A kidney? Like the organ?"

She sniffled and said, "Yes. Tess is in the house right now. They took her kidney."

Her words sank home and I felt an unbridled rage. I stood up, my hands shaking, and Jennifer saw the slide. She said, "Hey, maybe it's time to call the police."

I snapped, "What police? The Folly Beach Police Department? I'm sure they'll run right over after we tell them that someone's harvesting organs. They'll put one patrol car on it, and he'll either get killed or leave, satisfied that nothing's wrong. The girls will still die."

I started pacing, and Jennifer said, "What about a SWAT team? We tell them what's going on, and they hit it with a SWAT team?"

"Jennifer, there is no Folly Beach SWAT team. The biggest thing they deal with is drunk assholes on the beach. If they have a SWAT team it's a bunch of part-timers that shoot just a little more than the average cop. They aren't up for this."

"So what do we do?"

I turned to her and said, "You know what we do. There aren't many people with the talent to help in this situation, but fortunately for Tess, it's in this room."

She nodded, getting her head around what I was asking, but not shying away. She said, "So?"

"So you go conduct a recce of the house. Figure out

the breach points and give me an assault plan. You get back here, and we go in."

There was no pushback, because she knew I was right, and I trusted her ability to conduct a close target reconnaissance. Despite her surfer-model looks and her continual smacking of my moral compass, she was a predator of the first order.

She left the room and I turned back to Beth, saying, "This will all be over soon."

"What happens if you lose?"

"We won't lose."

She hesitated, then said, "Okay, but just say that happens. What then?"

I said, "You're free."

I took the keys to my Jeep out of my pocket and placed them in her hands, saying, "If we're not back by morning, you take the Jeep and go wherever you want to."

She stared at the keys and said, "I wish my father was like you. He never came."

Honestly, I was unsure of her situation. For all I knew, her father had abused her from the time she was six. He might have been as bad as Slaven.

I said, "Do you love him?"

And she started crying, saying, "Yes, yes, yes."

I put my arm around her and said, "Then don't worry about having to use those keys. Trust me, he's trying to find you. I was just lucky. I'll be back, and you'll see him soon. All I ask is you keep an eye on my daughter until I return."

Chapter 14

AN HOUR LATER, I was crouched in the shadows next door to the target house, the darkness cloaking my body, my finger on the safety of an integrally suppressed AR platform chambered in 300 Blackout, the barrel loosely aimed at Slaven's head to my right. I heard, "This is Koko. Climbing now."

I said, "Roger. Copy." I nodded at Slaven and said, "It's almost game time. Remember what we talked about. If you want to live, you'll follow instructions."

Jennifer's reconnaissance had taken less than thirty minutes, as the target was literally under a mile away. She'd come back and given me a complete dump on the house. A two-story structure built on stilts to protect from storm surges, with the bottom an open-air facility to park cars, it had a stairwell that went straight up to the front door and a balcony that circled the entire building, letting the renters sit out and watch the sun set over the ocean.

Apparently built sometime in the eighties, the house was older than others on Folly Beach, and as such didn't have any landscaping like most of the McMansion beach houses to the left and right, making sneaking up problematic. The good news was that because of the lack of foliage, it also didn't have the requisite landscaped lighting, either, leaving the house shrouded in darkness.

Amena and Beth told us that there were four men in the house, three who'd recently arrived from Myrtle Beach and looked like killers, and the fourth the one they called the doctor. The asshole that did the makeshift surgery for the exit fee. I was really hoping that guy cowered when we hit the place, because I wanted to give him some pain besides a bullet to the head.

The one edge we had was that the men had no idea we were coming and were probably comfortable in their security. I didn't think they'd have a guard force armed and ready. If we hit the house from two opposite breach points at the same time, we might be able to dominate them. The beachfront balcony at the back I gave to Jennifer. It had no stairwell, but she could climb like a monkey, getting eyes on the interior of the house so I didn't have to worry about that side of the building. I would take the front door.

Even given that they probably weren't pulling active security, I had to project what *I* would do in their shoes, and I had to assume they were all armed and had a camera out, looking at anyone who approached from the street. We needed a shield to lull them. Someone who would project a sense of belonging.

Fortunately, we had such a thing, and his name was Slaven.

After we'd built our assault plan, I'd smacked him around a little bit and then told him his role: Get to the front door, get it open, and then just curl into a ball, giving me a shot at whoever answered. I had no illusions about his loyalty, which meant I knew he cared about his own skin more than anything else. I knew I'd enter the house with him to my rear, but he had no weapons, and I figured he'd just begin sprinting down the street. Honestly, I didn't care. If he got away, so be it. My focus was on the women in the house.

We'd dropped Jennifer off a block away so she could infiltrate along the beach, then had parked on a side street, going on foot to the edge of the target house's lawn. I used the neighbor's bushes for concealment and waited on Jennifer's call that the back was secure.

Two minutes after her initial climbing call I heard, "I'm up. On the balcony. I can see inside. Light's on, three men. No females."

I said, "Understand. Koko, you ready to get bloody?"

I heard nothing for a moment, and I waited. My words weren't bravado. I meant it, because we were about to start splitting skulls, and I needed to make sure that

Jennifer was in. If she hesitated on the trigger—if she had a doubt—someone would die. And I didn't want that someone to be me.

She came back on, and I heard the steel in her voice. She said, "Yeah, I'm ready."

Slaven looked at me, and I nodded, seating my weapon to my shoulder, centering the holosight on his head. I said, "I can hit a dime from this distance. Just follow the plan."

He threaded through the bushes, then walked across the lawn and went up the steps. He reached the top, and like it was slow motion, I saw his hand stretch out to the doorbell. He punched it, and a moment later the door swung wide.

I'd told him to do nothing but get the door open and then step aside, giving me a shot at the man who answered. I'd impressed on him that anything otherwise would constitute his death. It appeared he was doing as I asked, and then he began speaking in a language I didn't understand, a staccato blurt to the man inside the house.

And I knew I had fallen for the easiest trap of warfare. Any time you initiate contact, the enemy gets a vote. Slaven was voting right in front of my eyes.

The man in the house pulled out a revolver and began waving his hands for Slaven to get inside. Slaven pointed out my position in the darkness, then tried to dodge away, getting out of the line of fire, but he made his choice.

Motherfucker.

The man in the doorway began shooting, but I ignored him, tracking Slaven. I broke the trigger twice, saw his head explode and his body slam to the ground, then focused on the door, putting an enormous amount of fire against it from twenty meters away, chipping wood and causing the man to fall back.

I pushed out of the bushes and rushed forward, knowing I needed the momentum, but realizing there was a slim chance I could get up the stairwell and breach without getting killed. Doorways were known as the funnel of death for a reason, because anyone entering was silhouetted. A perfect target, especially when surprise was lost.

I crouched at the base of the stairs and shouted into the radio, "Koko, Koko, I can't make breach, I can't make breach."

I heard nothing.

I trained my weapon on the open door. The man from inside made the mistake of jumping out, looking for a shot at my old position. I gave him a double tap, flinging him back into the door frame. Before his body had even hit the ground I heard more rounds coming out the breach point, bullets snapping by my head. Someone else was shooting, and this time they knew where I was located.

I dove underneath the stairs, then heard the dist crack of a suppressed rifle, followed by a rapid stri rounds inside the house.

Jennifer.

I rolled out and started sprinting up the stairs, my weapon leading the way, wanting to make breach and join the battle, my terror of leaving Jennifer alone in a gunfight overcoming any fear of a funnel of death.

My radio came to life, "Front breach clear. I say again, front breach clear. I'm moving."

I entered, leaping over a body and seeing Jennifer scanning the room, a dead man at her feet.

Holy shit. She killed both of them.

I tapped her on the shoulder and said, "Three down. One to go. Let me lead."

She said, "Slaven?"

"He's dead too. So it's four now. Let's go."

She nodded, ducked her barrel to let me get in front, and we started clearing one room at a time. The ground floor was empty. I raced up the stairs, Jennifer right behind me, and reached a door. I waited, felt Jennifer's hand on my shoulder, and shattered the doorknob with my foot, swinging it open.

I saw a girl on a bed, an intravenous tube snaking to her arm, her eyes wide open in fear. Behind her was a slender man holding another woman with a gun against her head. He wasn't like the men we'd killed at the restaurant or inside the house. He was weak-looking, with a pasty face and a thin goatee. He wasn't a predator. I trained my holosight on his skull and he shouted, "I'll kill her! I'll kill her!"

I lowered my weapon and said, "Are you the doctor?"

He didn't reply, but I saw the surprise in his eyes at the name. I felt a flash of anger that I fought to control. I wanted to punish him like few men I'd ever met, and I'd met some serious assholes, sending them to their grave with immense pain, but I didn't have the time for that here. I needed to free the girl, and that meant I needed to give him a reason to quit.

I said again, "Are you the doctor? Are you the one who took the kidney?"

He said, "Are you with Vlado?"

I nodded, and he dropped the pistol to his side, saying, "Yes, yes, I'm the doctor. What's wrong? You should have gotten the kidney. It was pristine. Why are you here?"

I exhaled my breath, lowered my pulse rate, brought my weapon to my shoulder, and broke the trigger, absorbing the recoil and watching the target through the scope. I saw the bullet enter his eye orbit, severing his medulla oblongata. He dropped, folding up on the ground like he had no bones in his body, his head on the floor, the front misshapen from the bullets and the back blown out completely.

The girl screamed and danced back, waving her hands in the air like that would make everything go away, the woman on the bed wailing in fear.

I said, "Jennifer, on her," and turned back to the doorway, clearing the hall and the final two rooms. Nobody else presented themselves.

I returned to the room, seeing Jennifer on the bed

next to the girl with the IV, whispering into her ear, her long gun on a sling dangling by her body like she was some insane mash-up of Dr. Laura and Lara Croft.

She looked up at me and I said, "House is clear. We need to go."

"How?" She nodded to the girl on the bed and said, "We can't leave her here." She pointed at the woman to her left, the one I'd just saved, and said, "We can't leave *her* here, and she's in shock."

I dropped my weapon on its sling and said, "We're not leaving anybody anywhere. Search that guy. Find his cell phone and call 911."

She nodded, went to the body, and found a smart phone. She held it up and said, "The clock will be ticking once I call."

I said, "Yeah, I know." I turned to the woman next to the bed, saw her moaning and trying to get the doctor's brain matter off of her face. I went to the bathroom, found a washcloth, and soaked it in water. I returned to her and said, "Calm down. It's okay."

I handed her the washcloth, and she nodded, nearly catatonic. She began rubbing the blood off of her face.

I said, "Your name is Misty, right?"

She paused, the rag in her hand against her cheek, surprised. She said, "Yes. How did you know?"

"I know a friend of yours. Beth. Are you like her? Is someone looking for you?"

She shook her head and said, "Nobody's looking for me. Nobody wants me."

And she started crying. I wasn't sure if it was because of what she'd just gone through or because she really felt that way, but I didn't have the time to figure it out. I did, however, have a couple of seconds to spare.

I pulled her close, wrapped my arms around her, and said, "That's not true. Family isn't blood. Amena made me come for you. Amena loves you. And so does Beth."

She looked up at me trying to find the lie, but didn't see one. She said, "I'm a whore. I've been a whore since I was fourteen."

I kissed her on the forehead and said, "Yesterday is yesterday. Tomorrow is tomorrow. Tomorrow you don't have to be a whore. You can be whatever you want."

She nodded and said, "What am I going to do? Where do I go?"

I said, "You don't have to figure that out right now. But if I were to give you some advice, I'd talk to Beth. Let her help you. Let her family help you."

She looked at me with a gallon's worth of wanting and said, "Do you think she will?"

I said, "I know she will."

Jennifer said, "Paramedics and cops are on the way. We need to leave."

I stood up, went to the woman in the bed, and said, "You'll be in a hospital soon. Don't worry. It's all going to work out."

She said, "Who are you?"

I looked at Jennifer, and she shook her head, knowing what was about to come out of my mouth. I couldn't resist.

I said, "I'm Batman."

The girl's eyes scrunched up, and I could see her brain trying to work through the drugs she'd been given. I winked and said, "I don't always wear a cape."

Jennifer rolled her eyes and I turned to Misty, saying "Hey, look, the police will be here soon. Tell them everything. Tell them everything that's happened. All I ask is that you not give them our physical descriptions. Don't give them anything they can use. Make it look like an opposing gang or something. Can you do that?"

She nodded, and I said, "Beth will call you, I promise. She'll help both of you."

She looked at Jennifer and said, "Can I say a woman was here? Can I at least do that? Tell them a woman killed these assholes?"

Jennifer smiled and said, "No, you can't. Please don't. It'll just cause questions."

I cocked my head, thought for a second, then said, "I don't give a shit. Tell 'em a killer came in, and she was female."

Jennifer's eyes snapped open, and I knew what she was thinking. Nobody knew about her, not even in the top-secret circles of the military or the intelligence community, and she liked it that way. She was a female who was better at operating than most of men in any unit in the United States arsenal. But because of her gender we made her live in the shadows. It really wasn't fair. A lot of people talked about women in the military and what they *might* be able to do, but Jennifer was *doing* it.

I winked at her, then turned to Misty, saying, "I'm sort of sick of getting the glory. Tell them it was Batwoman."

Chapter 15

SITTING ON THE floor of our house four days later, Amena said, "Okay, okay, everyone be quiet."

She'd finally convinced me to watch the stupid *Game of Thrones* show and had cornered us in the living room with a giant bowl of popcorn. I had no idea what was happening in the series, but I figured I could watch at least one episode. I mean, hell, it was sort of embarrassing that a Syrian refugee knew more about American pop culture than I did.

The screen went through about a five-minute intro with something like a Lego set coming to life, wasting my time. I said, "Why am I watching this? I don't know what's going on. I'm not going to understand it."

Amena hissed, "This is the one with Arya. Don't talk."

Jennifer snickered, snuggled into my arms on the couch, and whispered, "Just watch it. Don't say anything."

Amena was transfixed on the screen, slowly putting popcorn in her mouth, and it made me smile.

It had been four days since the actions at Slaven's house, and so far we were in the clear. Nobody in an official capacity had made any connection to us, so I began to believe that Misty had taken my words to heart. The only thing on the news was that some crazy-ass woman had ripped through the place slaughtering everyone, and then had vanished.

It had been repeated breathlessly on the local stations, which gave Jennifer no small amount of smugness, but it hadn't gone anywhere. The girl in the bed—Tess—had been transported to a hospital, where they'd found the beginnings of sepsis. One more day in that bed, and she'd have died.

The news also talked about the two dead men in Rita's, and speculation was ripe that it was connected to the death house, but the police simply fell back to saying the investigation was "ongoing."

I'd have liked to leave it all alone, but in the end, I'd had to tell Kurt Hale what I'd done. Not because I felt like confessing, but because Beth had said Slaven was using her to turn a man working at the naval nuke school. She'd told me Slaven had leveraged her to force him to provide information for later sale, and I'd searched his phone, finding that he had, in fact, sent contact information for a meeting.

That was more than I could resolve by myself. I'd contacted Kurt Hale and told him what I had. Which is a short sentence for what ended up being a very, very long conversation. In the end, I'd convinced him that I wasn't, in fact, a lunatic, and that there had been a penetration of the Naval Nuclear Power Training School. He'd washed my connection to the information, contacted the right people from the FBI, and I'd gone to the meet site—a Mexican restaurant called Taco Boy on Huger Street.

Taking a seat on the outside deck, the tables around me full of FBI agents, I honestly hoped that Lannister wouldn't show. Praying he'd decided his career wasn't worth treason.

But he had.

I saw him at the entrance and felt a little sadness. He recognized me from the parking garage and had come right over. He'd said, "Okay, I couldn't get much, but I got some stuff."

I'd said, "Where is it?"

He'd passed across a thumb drive and said, "That's the maintenance records for the last six months."

I palmed it and said, "This had better not be a bunch of shit from the motor pool."

He glanced left and right, then looked at me, saying, "It's not. Trust me. We're done now, right?"

I nodded and said, "Oh yeah, we're done."

I stood up and walked away. Twenty agents descended on him, slamming him into the table. I passed the thumb drive to the lead agent at the door and he said, "Thanks. We appreciate it."

I said, "No problem."

He palmed the thumb drive, paused, then said, "If you don't mind me asking, who do you work for?"

Seeing Lannister McBride facedown on the table, a flurry of agents around him, and feeling the sleaze of the last three days, I said, "A Syrian refugee. That's who."

I saw his eyes cloud in confusion and left him there, walking to my car. Inside were Jennifer and Amena.

I got in the passenger seat feeling tired and dirty. I said, "Let's go. Take me away from here."

Jennifer did so and Amena said, "So you got the bad man?"

I said, "Yeah. I got the bad man."

"Beth will be happy."

And that brought a smile. Because she was right.

After the assault, we'd returned to the sleazy hotel and had rapidly packed up, cleansing anything that could point to us. Amena had asked a ton of questions and Beth had acted like she was unsure of her fate. We didn't have the time to sort out anything right then because we'd left a houseful of dead people that was about to be ground zero for the greatest news story Folly Beach had ever seen.

I'd taken Beth in my car, and Jennifer had taken Amena, both of us driving back to our house on the peninsula.

During the drive, Beth had asked, "What are you going to do with me now?"

I'd passed her my cell phone and said, "Quit that. We already talked about what's next. Call your father. Tell him you're coming home."

Stunned, she'd just looked at me. I said, "No tricks. Call him."

She'd picked up the phone like it was going to explode and said, "You're going to let me call whoever I want?"

I'd said, "Yes. As long as it's your family. If he's like me, he's begging to hear from you. Like I was with Amena."

She said, "I haven't been allowed to talk on a phone that Slaven didn't own since forever." She dialed, but I could tell she was afraid to speak. When someone answered, she said, "Daddy? Is that you?"

And then the waterworks had started. By the time I'd reached my home she was blubbering so hard I doubt anyone on the other end could understand what she was saying. I'd parked behind Jennifer, and Beth hung up, staring at me.

I said, "We have a couch for you tonight. Sorry, I don't have a spare bedroom."

She wrapped her arms around my neck and squeezed, saying, "I don't know what to say. I don't know what to give you."

I hugged her back and said, "You gave me Amena."

She'd sniffled, then nodded, unsure what to do next. I said, "But if you really want to pay me back, maybe you can give Misty a little help. I don't think she has a family like you do."

She'd nodded her head so hard I thought she was going to break her neck. She'd spent one night in Amena's bed—Amena saying she'd sleep on the couch—and we'd taken her to the airport with a ticket I'd purchased for Colorado.

It had been a little emotional at the drop-off, with her breaking down yet again and Jennifer beginning to do the same. I'd hugged her and said, "Remember what we talked about. Just like Misty, you can say whatever you want, but don't give away our identity. Just say you escaped from the motel."

Beth had asked not to be identified to the police right away, and I'd honored that request. She'd said she'd contact them after she was home and I didn't see a problem with it. After all, it wasn't like there was anyone left to prosecute, and Misty had been in captivity longer than Beth. All Beth would be doing was confirming the information Misty told them.

She'd laughed through the tears and said, "I don't even know your real name. I don't know anything about you."

I said, "You know enough to cause problems."

"Why is saving me a problem? You should be on the news as a hero."

Amena said, "He doesn't like the spotlight. I don't know why, either."

Beth bent down and hugged her, saying, "He's a pretty cool guy, huh?"

Amena took Jennifer's hand and said, "Yeah, they're both pretty cool. For old people."

Beth grinned, then turned to me a final time. She hugged me, squeezing hard, and said, "I'll keep in touch with Misty and Tess. They've got the police stuff to sort out here, and Tess will be in the hospital for a few weeks. but my dad says they can come stay when they're done."

I said, "I appreciate you helping them out. I'm sure they do as well."

She said, "My dad's starting a nonprofit to help people like me."

"He is?"

She shyly smiled and said, "Yeah, I didn't tell you before, but he's sort of rich. He asked me to help."

I grinned and said, "I think you'll be perfect at that. Better than perfect. You're the only one who knows what happens. You can save others who are lost."

The shyness dropped away and she nodded fiercely, saying, "That's exactly what I'm going to do."

I was surprised at how quickly her courage had returned, given what I'd seen in the motel. It was a good sign. Jennifer pulled her close and said, "You can free more of them than we ever did, that's for sure. Tell your dad that. Don't quit."

She said, "I'll never, *ever* quit."

And I knew she meant it.

She'd hugged Jennifer and then was gone, inside the airport and on her way to restart her life.

Two days later, I was being forced to watch a series about medieval folks on an ice wall bitching about the winter coming. But I had to admit, I liked Amena's fascination with the show. I pulled Jennifer into me and felt content.

Then I saw some guy having sex with his sister next to a dead body, right on our television.

I snapped upright, flinging Jennifer off of me, and said, "What the hell are we watching?"

Amena turned to me and said, "What?"

I snapped up the remote, saying, "No, no, no, *no*." I looked at Jennifer and said, "Did you know that stuff was happening on the show?"

She shook her head, saying, "I had no idea."

Amena said, "Put it back on!"

I said, "No, that's not going back on. You can see it when you're older."

She leapt up and said, "Pike! Put it back on."

"No. It's not going back on. You're done with that series. Winter has come and gone."

She scowled, crossed her arms over her chest, and I saw the war coming, like had happened six days ago. Jennifer gave her a gentle look and the scowl fell away.

Amena smiled and said, "Okay, Pike. Okay."

Surprised, I said, "Really?"

She'd never wanted to listen to me before, always fighting anything I'd asked, like she was an outsider being forced to bend to my will. Now, she was bending all on her own. It was a breakthrough.

Amena looked at Jennifer, then me, and said, "Yes. Because you're family. And I'll never fight my family again."

If you enjoyed *Exit Fee*,
keep reading for a sneak peek at the next
action-packed thriller by Brad Taylor,

Hunter Killer

Available in hardcover
Winter 2020 from William Morrow

Chapter 1

THE ROAD IN front of me was empty. Just a narrow alley leading to the entryway I intended to penetrate. A fetid, cobblestone lane built centuries ago, it was dimly lit, with more shadows than light and piles of trash hiding what may lie within.

Anywhere else in the world I would have silently cheered at the luck, but here, in Salvador, it raised the hackles on my neck. Empty roads in Brazil were like hearing the wildlife in a jungle suddenly go quiet, all the birds and monkeys realizing there was a predator afoot.

I was in the historical section of the old capital city, with plenty of folks less than a hundred meters away at restaurants and bars, but nobody was walking down this alley. Meaning there was a reason for the lack of activity. It was counterintuitive to anything I'd felt before, where the bystanders were most often the threat. Crowds allowed camouflage for individual hostiles, like pickpockets, but more important to me, they prevented offensive actions by a team.

There were just too many cameras and cell phones in today's world, devices that recorded an event no matter how careful one was, so an empty alley was the perfect approach for me, and yet, I'd learned in my short time in Brazil that empty meant dangerous. For some reason, the humans here knew not to enter, an instinct that I should pay attention to.

Unfortunately, that was out of the question because a bad guy, my target, held my best friend's life in the balance.

I turned to Aaron, and said, "That damn alley is going to be trouble. I can feel it."

He knew what I meant. We didn't worry about the "trouble," per se; we worried about the mission, and whatever was waiting for us there could hinder that.

He said, "Hey, we only have twelve hours before the clock is up. That's a blink of an eye for hostage rescue. We need to go tonight, or we're not stopping what the police have in motion."

I said, "Shoshana seems to think this is bad juju because of the monks. Maybe she's right."

He chuckled and said, "My wife is a little off. Like you."

I nodded, but still hesitated, running through my options. He squinted his eyes and said, "You believe her. You think this is going to go bad because of what she felt."

I said, "Aaron, cut the crap. She's crazy all right, but sometimes she has a point. That's all."

He withdrew a Glock pistol, press-checked the chamber, and said, "One way or the other, we need to make a decision. And I think you're afraid of her saying 'I told you so' because of this alley."

I grunted a laugh and said, "Yeah, something like that. But you're right. Too late now."

I clicked my earpiece and said, "Koko, Koko, I'm about to penetrate. What's your status?"

Koko was the callsign of my partner in crime, Jennifer, so named because she could climb like a monkey. She said, "I'm good. On the roof over the balcony. The OP is in position, and I have a clear shot."

"Roger, all. Carrie, Carrie, you have lockdown of the front?"

Carrie was Shoshana's callsign. Because she was batshit crazy just like the Stephen King character.

Ironically, the man I was working to save had anointed both of them with their callsigns. Which is why they were both willing to risk their lives to free him. They loved him as much as I did.

She came back, "This is Carrie. Front is secure. But I still think this is a mistake. We should not be assaulting a church. It's bad. Bad all the way around."

I looked at Aaron and said, "Yeah, I agree, but I don't get to pick where terrorists stay. I just wipe out the nest, wherever that ends up."

She said, "It's not the church itself. It's something else."

I took that in, then looked down the alley. I said, "You want to help here? I think I have your bad feeling, too."

She said nothing on the net. Aaron whispered, "Good call. The front is facing the tourists. She's not needed out there. Get her in play."

Through a combination of means, we'd tracked our target to the back of an old convent tacked on to a UNESCO World Heritage Site. Called the São Francisco Church, it had existed since the sixteenth century, with an ornate Gothic façade that now was the anchor of a square housing outdoor cafes and art galleries.

The front of the church—and the square it faced—was a completely safe place for tourists in the old capital of Salvador, but just outside the light, down the cobblestone streets we were on, the predators prowled, waiting on a stray lamb to leave the lights and laughter.

I took a look down the dimly lit alley, seeing the narrow confines of the ancient street snaking down the left-hand wall of the church, reconsidering whom I was asking for help. I'd left Shoshana to pull security within the crowds of tourists for a reason.

Off the net, to Aaron, I said, "I'm not sure that's so smart. She's better protecting us defensively. Out front. Away from the action."

Aaron said, "Because you don't trust her offensively?"

"You're damn right. She's a walking disaster. Better for Jennifer to do it."

"Jennifer's on the roof. Shoshana's perfect for this and you know it. Jennifer would be better as bait, with her blond hair and innocence, but Shoshana's the next-best thing."

He turned away for a moment, then looked me in the eye, saying, "Shoshana's a killer, but she's pure. She won't do anything if it's not warranted. Honestly, I'm more concerned about you."

Aaron had seen what I was capable of, and he was hitting at the core of the mission. Could I maintain control? It was a good question, because in an earlier life, he'd almost killed me, and in so doing, he'd killed a friend of mine. The results hadn't been pretty. He'd seen what I was capable of when I was walking the edge, leaning way over, and now I was operating in that same zone. Something he knew about.

I said, "I'm good. Don't worry about me. Just worry about the threat."

He nodded, but I could see he wasn't convinced.

Shoshana came back on the net, whispering with an urgency neither Aaron nor I understood, "You feel something too, Nephilim?"

Aaron grinned, and I returned it, holding up a finger before he got on the net. I said, "Yeah, but it's not because of some damn ancient church. It's because I can't get to entry. I don't want a gunfight. I need quiet, which means I need you."

"So you want me to do what?"

"Walk down this alley from the back. Expose any threat that may prevent our entry."

She said nothing for a moment, then came back, "That's what you want? Me as bait?"

Aaron's eyes widened, and I saw him reaching to key his mike, him saying, "That's not how to get her to execute."

I held up my hand again and beat him to the punch, saying, "Carrie, this is the threat. *This* is what I feel. And this is what I need."

Aaron and I looked at each other, and I felt my cell phone vibrate in my pocket. Shoshana came back on and said, "This is Carrie. I'm moving to the south of the alley. I'll be coming south to north. I'll have the light on my phone going."

I pulled out my cell, saw it was Jennifer, and realized she didn't want to talk on the open net. I held it up, then whispered to Aaron, "Tell Shoshana that all we need is to flush out any threats. We'll handle it. I don't need any crazy shit here. She just walks toward us until someone triggers. Or until she reaches us without a trigger."

Aaron nodded and I answered the phone, saying, "What?"

Jennifer said, "You're going to let Shoshana loose in that alley, after you felt a threat? Let's back off. Attack a different way."

I saw a pinpoint of light at the back of the alley and said, "Too late. She's in."

Jennifer said, "That's a bad call. She'll kill anyone who threatens her."

I said, "If it's the guys that we're hunting, I don't give a shit."

She said, "Pike, don't go there—"

And I hung up, watching the light. Not wanting to think about what I'd just said. Not after what had happened to my friend. She knew where I was headed, because she'd seen it once before. I knew it, too.

The difference was I wanted it.

The light bounced down the alley until it was abreast of our entry point, and Aaron and I began slinking down the lane, hiding from the streetlights behind us, stepping over the trash to avoid the noise. We closed the gap, both wound as tight as a tripwire, waiting. And it came.

Two men assaulted Shoshana from both sides of the alley, one from behind a dumpster and the other from a gap in the bricks.

They slammed into her in a synchronized assault, and we took off running, reaching them just as they gained the upper hand. I saw one man cinch his hand into Shoshana's hair, then bash her skull into the cobblestones. The second had his arms wrapped around her legs, pulling out a blade that glinted in the moonlight.

They were in total control, right up until we reached them. Aaron slammed his boot into the man holding her hair and I jumped on the man holding her legs. I caught a glimpse of their fight, and then was subsumed with my own.

He began attacking me, attempting to hammer my face with elbows and fists, and then hit me with the knife in my forearm. I blocked the initial blows, returned them with my own, then felt the blade slice through my jacket, nicking my flesh.

The wound he caused split open the blackness, the anger inside me boiling out. I gave him everything I'd bottled up over the last week. I abandoned my "team leader control" and let the beast run free, looking for vengeance.

I battered his face, trapped his wrist against his torso, the blade now useless, circled around his body, and wrapped him up in my arms, pressing his head forward into his chest. He began frothing at the mouth, flailing his one good fist, and then gave up, dropping the knife and raising his other hand in an effort to surrender. It did no good. I wanted a release, and I worked to achieve it. I pressed him further, going deeper, until I felt his neck snap.

The sound split through the pain, jerking me out of my darkness. I let him sink to the ground, looking at Shoshana and Aaron. Both were staring back at me, Shoshana holding the other attacker in a joint lock, facedown on the ground.

She said, "You were worried about me going crazy? What was that?"

I shook my head, clearing the beast, not sure what I'd done. I said, "Let's go. Put him out."

She nodded, then asked, "Permanently?"

Because that's just how she thinks.

Not liking what I'd just done, I said, "No. Not permanently."

She said, "He's Russian. He's not a common predator. He's here for *you*."

For the first time, I noticed that the man I'd fought wasn't from Brazil. I searched him, finding a passport from Saint Kitts. The same passport I'd found on the Russian I'd killed in Charleston. The one who had murdered my friend.

The blackness came rushing back.

This is all tied together. And it ends now.

She looked at me expectantly, and I closed my eyes, reliving the explosion and the charred body.

Shoshana said, "Pike?"

I locked eyes with Aaron, and he didn't flinch, just stared at me, letting me make the choice. Not judging in any way.

A part of me wanted to call Jennifer. Wanting someone to stop the slide I was on. She was the only one who could prevent it. I didn't. Like a junkie feeling the heroin, I enjoyed what I was doing.

I stepped over the edge of the abyss.

"Kill him."

Chapter 2

One Week Ago

NUNG HEARD HIS boss swear out loud and shout, "Nung! Get your ass out here."

He stopped packing several laptops and rose from a pelican case. He tossed in some bubble wrap and strode to the front of the company's makeshift do-it-yourself office, more of a trailer than a structure. He opened the aluminum door, feeling the oppressive humidity of Myanmar hit and begin to soak his shirt, a relentless cycle that didn't faze him, unlike the men he worked for. Being from Thailand, he had long ago ceased caring about the sweat/air conditioner sequence, but the men who'd hired him despised the furnace of Myanmar. He poked his head out and saw his boss attempting to talk in sign language to a Burmese official. Meaning they were doing nothing but waving their arms.

His boss saw him and shouted, "Come on. Get over here."

He called himself Domingo, but Nung didn't believe that was his boss's name, because he knew the man was from Russia. Well, he didn't *know* Domingo was from Russia, but the fact that he spoke Russian was an indicator. The subterfuge wasn't particularly alarming to Nung, as he'd spent most of his life straddling the gray area between legal and illegal. In the end, Nung hadn't questioned the name because he, himself, was operating under the same subterfuge—his name wasn't Nung, the Thai word for "one," just as his brother wasn't named Song, for the Thai word for "two." The similarities, though, ended at the use of an alias, because Nung took his job seriously, wanting to earn his pay.

Unlike Domingo.

Nung reached the scrum, seeing Domingo's false eye staring off into space, something that was always disconcerting to him. He never understood why the man didn't wear a patch—or at least make sure his eye was looking forward. He heard Domingo say to the other contractor, in Russian, "This idiot is as bad as the dumbasses we were hired to help. Thank God this contract is over."

Nung showed no emotion. The men he worked with had no idea he understood Russian, and he wanted to keep it that way. He'd learned plenty about their operations over the past four months on the contract, and all of it could be lucrative for his father and family.

A lithe man of just under six feet, he was taller than most Thais because of his heritage. His father wa

American—a Caucasian who'd flown for Air America out of Thailand during the secret war in Laos and Cambodia, where he'd worked more than just an aircraft for the CIA. After the war had ended, his father had stayed in Thailand, using the contacts he'd developed during the war to create a black market empire in the seedy underbelly of Bangkok. He'd married a Thai, and had raised his sons in the family business. Because of it, Nung had grown up—not *immoral*, but certainly amoral.

His father had owned a brothel in the famed Patpong red-light district, which catered to foreign nationals. Unlike the other brothels that trafficked in underage boys and rough sex, he'd trafficked in exotic women. Russians, Swedes, Ukrainians. You name it, he had them.

Nung grew up in that world, so much that when his mother had died when he was at the age of four, he'd been raised by a Russian nanny. A woman his father had taken a liking to and had pulled out of the lineup for a softer life. She'd shown a greater intelligence than most his father had brought over, but the winning attribute was a true affection for his sons.

The woman had been his life for years while his father worked, never acting as if she was doing anything for money, showing what he had later learned was love. A strange concept he'd never understood as a child, given his father's transactional life.

She was killed in a car accident after Nung had gone to a university, but her lasting legacy had been a touch-

stone of caring that was the only bit of emotion he had. Well, that and the fact he could speak Russian. Something he kept hidden from his current employer.

He knew that Domingo had no idea, the thought fanciful. How could a Thai hired to work in Myanmar speak Russian?

But he did.

In English, the chosen language between them, Nung said, "What's the problem?"

Domingo said, "The problem is I can't tell what this idiot is asking. We were told to clear out of this camp now that it's operational but he wants to keep our sensors. That's not happening. He wants them, he can buy his own."

Nung worked for a group of Russians called Wagner, a private military contractor from the Russian Federation that had been hired by the government of Myanmar to help with the repatriation of the Rohingya, a persecuted group who had fled from a genocidal effort by the government to eradicate them from existence.

They were a Muslim subset of the population of Myanmar, with its own language and customs, and the government had tried to kill them off for years, but really ramped up efforts in 2017, in a concerted attempt to cause them to flee or die, a final solution.

After the rapes, murders, and burning of villages, the government got what they wanted; the Rohingya fled to Bangladesh, like they'd done for decades before, but this time it had a new twist; the world was more connected, and the atrocities were caught on the internet. It was, in fact, a genocide.

Embarrassed, the government of Myanmar had begun trotting out a hundred excuses for what had occurred, and offered to repatriate the ones who'd fled. And that was where Nung came in.

Now wanting to look like the good guys, the government had begun receiving the people back into the Rakhine State, albeit into refugee camps because their homes had been burned to the ground by government troops. Wagner had been contracted to build the camps. And they needed local help.

Nung, because he spoke the language, had been hired through his father's contacts to interact with the Burmese. It wasn't lost on him that even though they'd reached out to his father for help, they were not as respectable as the Red Cross.

He didn't mind, though. He could take the insults and the less-than-noble actions he witnessed Wagner conduct. It was all business.

Until it wasn't.

Nung saw Domingo push the man, then said, "What's the problem? Let it go. Those sensors were paid for by the contract. You've already made the money on them."

"Bullshit. That's wrong. They paid for my services. If they want the sensors, then they need to buy their own. Tell him he's fucked."

Nung said some words to the official, and he began waving his arms again, incensed. Domingo slapped the Burmese official's hands out of the air, and Nung considered translating the wrong way and causing a fight. He'd seen how the Burmese treated the Rohingya, and it wasn't as pure as the state propaganda machine put out. The man in front of him was just as bad as the man behind him. They were both evil, and it would be nice to see them destroy each other.

He did not.

In short order, he had the situation resolved, the Burmese official walking away in a huff. He turned to the Russian and said, "Continue packing?"

Domingo said, "Yeah. I want to be out of this shithole in the next four hours. Let them deal with it now."

Two hours later, Nung finished sealing the rest of the office equipment while Domingo and the other man talked in the shallow office to his left. As usual, they were speaking in Russian, and as usual, Nung was listening. He didn't really care what they did with the Rohingya, because he was paid for a service, and he provided it. But in his heart he did. He hated the Russians because of what he'd seen. They hadn't done a damn thing to really help the refugees because the government hadn't cared. It was all a joke for the press.

The Rohingya members had been abused and castigated from the moment they'd created the first camp, and nobody seemed to give a damn, least of all the

Russians of Wagner—which was the express purpose the Russians had hired him: helping to facilitate the re-settlement of the refugees. It aggravated him. He could deal with the blood and violence, because he'd done it himself, but it was always against an enemy who understood the rules. Not a bunch of families that were being persecuted solely because of their heritage.

He'd called his father only once, and had been told to continue, because the Russian connection was a good one, and he'd been forced to choose. Family meant everything to him. There was no allegiance beyond that. Family was all. And so he'd continued. But he held a growing hatred, and while they treated him as the hired local help, they had no idea of his skills.

Luckily for them, they'd never see it, and he could finally go home, serving his father and expanding the family business.

Shoving more bubble wrap into another pelican case, Nung heard Domingo talking on a phone in the next room. He heard discussions about an operation in Brazil, and then Domingo became heated with the man on the phone, saying his men were already there and they couldn't afford another compromise like the one in France.

Nung perked up, no longer packing the case. Domingo glanced out of the door and said, "No, nobody can hear me. I'm working with savages."

Then he said, "Are you sure? The same ones who killed Tagir? They're in Brazil?"

Nung worked around the box, pretending to pack but really moving closer to the door. He heard, "Yeah, I got the email. I'm looking at it right now. Are you asking what to do? I'll tell you what to do. Cut the head off of the snake. You know where he is. You got the information for Grolier Services, right?"

Nung heard the words and had to physically stop himself from showing a reaction. Domingo continued, "I don't care who they saw in Brazil, you kill that fuck in Charleston, and it'll end. Get it done."

He heard the phone slam, then Domingo stormed out of the office, looking at Nung and saying, "What the hell is taking so long? Pack that shit up."

Nung said, "What's the rush? We've been here for four months."

Domingo said, "It looks like I'm going to Brazil, and I need to leave immediately. Get it done."

Nung nodded, watching him stomp out of the trailer. As soon as the door had closed, he went into the small office where Domingo had talked. The one with the desktop computer he was not allowed to access. He saw the window on the computer was open, the time-out for the password not yet engaged.

He went to email. He glanced behind him, seeing the outside door still closed. He pulled up the first email and saw nothing but Cyrillic lettering. He cursed under his breath.

While he'd learned to speak Russian, he couldn't read it. He highlighted all of it, then pasted it into Google

Translate. The words that came out were a little schizo-phrenic, like an old telegram, but there was enough for him to make out:

> The group highlight in Switzerland be highlight in Brazil. Two members seen in Salvador. Cannot stop say who else is involved. But military contract people not people might prevent success. Presidential campaign is reaching apex and that though Lulu oilfields are in doubt. Recommend another Op-eration Harvest. Target Grolier Recovery Services now, before they harvest operation.

Nung read the words, and inwardly curled. What he'd heard earlier was correct. They were after Grolier Services. He had no idea why, but it made him bristle.

He heard the door slam open outside, and closed down the Google Translate page. He went outside the small office and saw Domingo glaring at him.

He said, "What?"

Domingo said, "What, what? What the fuck are you doing? Pack this shit up. I want to go."

"I was looking at preparing the desktop in your office."

"Don't touch that. I'll do that myself. I have to use the sat dish to get some plane tickets. Those fucks in Moscow want me to fly tonight. It never ends."

Nung said, "To Charleston, in the United States?"

"Fuck no, someone else is doing the easy work. I have to go to Moscow, then Brazil." And then something clicked in Domingo's brain. "How the fuck do you know about Charleston?"

Nung reverted to what Domingo knew; a dumb-ass savage. He ducked his head in supplication and said, "When you were on the phone, the only word I heard you say in English was Charleston. I'll get this packed up soon."

Domingo nodded, staring at him for a beat. Nung knew for all his bluster, he was not a dumb man. He'd seen it over five months. Nung bent down to the closest pelican case, packing up office equipment, and waited, feeling his eyes on him.

After five brutal seconds, Domingo left, shouting at his men. And Nung made his decision.

He knew the man who owned Grolier Recovery Services. He knew what that man had done for his younger brother. And he knew that only one thing counted in this world.

Family.

Something Domingo would learn the hard way.

Chapter 3

AMENA FOUND ME in the bathroom and said, "Why do you pick such fights? This is supposed to be a party."

Looking in the mirror, and honestly a little embarrassed at my actions, I said, "Because it's just some friends coming over. We don't need to turn this into a New Year's Eve gala."

She caught my eye in the reflection and said, "So you guys are fighting because you don't want to work? Is that it?"

I turned from the mirror, and she continued, "I'm not saying you're wrong. I'm just trying to learn what to expect here in America."

I knew she was toying with me, because she was smart as a whip and had picked up "being American" within a few weeks of arrival, now acting like any other thirteen-year-old teenager.

Amena was a refugee from Syria who had done some good deeds for America. Well, that's putting it lightly. She'd saved a ton of lives, all because she thought it was the right thing to do, risking her own life and almost giving it in the process. And because of it, I'd saved hers, bringing her to the United States.

Taller than an average thirteen-year-old, with tan skin, black hair, and black eyes, she was beautiful in an exotic sort of way. Her looks caused tourists to comment when we were out and about on the peninsula, asking where she was from, which initially aggravated the hell out of me. I was trying to protect her status, and some bloated lady from a cruise ship would act like she wanted to pet the strange animal. I took it as an insult, but Amena never did. She thought it was a compliment, and honestly, she *was* something exotic. In more ways than one.

Playacting like she was trying to determine how a man and woman behaved in America, she was really trying to cool the fight, because she was torn between loving me or loving Jennifer. She wanted us both.

I turned to her and said, "No, this isn't how it is in America. I'm just being an asshole."

She giggled and said, "Then why do you do it?"

"Because I'm stubborn."

She nodded and said, "I know. Now what?"

I sighed and said, "Now I have to eat crow."

And I'd finally said something American that made no sense to Amena. She scrunched her eyes and said, "Eat crow? Like a bird?"

I said, "It's just a saying that means I have to go admit I was wrong. How about you go out there and assist? With something too big for you to do? And then you come back here and ask me to help?"

She caught on immediately and raced out, wanting to end any disagreement between her hero, Jennifer, and me. Wanting to get back to the affection that gave her a blanket of security. Thirty seconds later, she was back, saying, "Can you help me with the tray of shrimp? It's too big for me to move."

I smiled, which brought out a grin of her own, and out we went.

I entered our living room, saw Jennifer scowling, and Amena said, "He's going to help me. Because I can't move it."

I looked at Jennifer and said, "I can't tell her no."

Jennifer's expression softened, and I knew she understood this was my way of giving in. She motioned me over, saying, "I could use some help as well."

I went to her, and she put her arms around my neck and kissed me on the lips. "It would be a lot easier if you just did the work, without the fighting."

I grinned and said, "I know."

Jennifer gave me a radiant smile back, melting any notion of contradicting whatever she wanted, and Amena practically broke the windows with her own beaming face, happy to have solved the dilemma.

Although deep inside, I *still* thought this was bullshit. All we should have been doing was packing.

Jennifer and I were slated for a mission in Brazil in a few days, hunting some Hezbollah financiers at the tri-border region, and normally such preparation would be old hat, but now we had Amena. We were working to find her a permanent home, but that took time.

Jennifer had come up with a stroke of brilliance, asking Kylie Hale, the niece of Kurt Hale, the commander of our unit, if she would house-sit while we were gone. Kylie had some history with Jennifer—meaning once upon a time, Jennifer had saved her life. She was currently wandering about trying to put her recent degree in English literature to use—meaning she was researching graduate schools—so she'd readily jumped at the chance to travel to Charleston for a salary that involved nothing more than watching Amena.

She'd arrived yesterday to become acquainted with our routine, and I thought we were set. Then she'd asked if her boyfriend could visit while we were gone. I didn't have a problem with that, because her boyfriend also happened to be on my team, and he was following Jennifer and me to Brazil shortly, so it wasn't like he could get in any trouble. I'd said fine, and she informed me he was coming today, suspiciously sounding like it had already been planned. Just to cap it off, later in the day, my commander, Colonel Kurt Hale, called and said he was passing through town and wanted to visit—which I knew was bullshit. Kurt was never just "passing through." There was an agenda in play, but with all three descending on our house, Jennifer had decided to throw a party, which made me grumpy.

Jennifer saw I was still less than enthusiastic and said, "Why don't you head to the store? I forgot a few things that I need for tonight. Amena and I can finish up here."

I jumped at the chance, snatching a grocery list out of her hand and racing toward the door.

"Take the Jeep," she said, "My car's blocked in." And I knew she was punishing me. It was only October, and Charleston should have still been a muggy swelter, but we'd had an early cold snap, making the air temperature about fifty degrees. She knew I hadn't replaced the top to the Jeep, and would therefore freeze while driving it.

I didn't care, because driving that beat-up CJ was better than her little Mini Cooper. It was my pride and joy—and a tax write-off, because it was our company vehicle, the rear quarter panel adorned with an emblem that said Grolier Recovery Services.

I climbed in, turned the old-fashioned key, and backed out our little drive, inching into the street while praying nobody slammed into me.

On the surface, Grolier Recovery Services helped facilitate archeological work around the world, and to that end, Jennifer and I made a pretty good living. We did about three jobs to one in the real world, working for various agencies that wanted the best at deciphering the mundane world of geopolitics and antiquities. The remaining job was what we really existed for—finding a bad guy and planting him in the ground, paid for courtesy of the United States government.

The cover work that facilitated our ability to conduct counterterrorism operations around the world had been pretty lucrative—enough to buy a small two-story row house on Wentworth Street just off East Bay on the Charleston Peninsula. It was a little fixer-upper with a narrow gravel drive on the side just big enough to fit three cars end to end. Jennifer and I were constantly rotating vehicles in and out, but the worst part was getting onto Wentworth Street from the blind alley.

I made it out okay and shot over to the Harris Teeter grocery store a couple of blocks away, getting out and reading the list. I immediately realized I should have checked it in Jennifer's presence, because it was full of inscrutable things that caused me to wander the store like a Buddhist monk searching for the secret to life, texting her questions about each item and sending pictures when necessary.

I knew she'd given up when I saw a FaceTime call from her. I answered and she said, "I'm not sure how you managed to make it through life not knowing how a supermarket works."

I said, "I know where the Doritos and beer are located. Sometimes the milk, but you're making me find a bunch of stuff with foreign-sounding names like Gruyère cheese. That stuff wasn't even in the cheese section."

She shook her head, saying, "Just come back with what you have. Kurt's already here. I'll go back out. You win."

I said, "I'm doing my best! I'm almost done."

She glanced away from the phone, and then leaned into the screen, whispering, "He wants to talk, so get your ass home."

I said, "About what?"

She glanced away again, making sure she was out of earshot and said, "I don't know, but I need you here for whatever it is, because I don't think it's good."

Chapter 4

As soon as she said it, I knew Kurt was here about Amena. And Jennifer knew that she wouldn't be able to fight whatever he was going to say, but I sure as shit could. It was sort of my specialty.

I nodded and said, "I'm on the way."

Kurt Hale and I had a unique relationship. On the one hand, he was my direct superior—the commander of Project Prometheus and the one who gave me my operational orders. On the other, we were almost as close as brothers, with a deep friendship that had lasted for decades. We'd first met when I was assigned to his troop in a special mission unit, and we had both been promoted up the ranks, serving together multiple times. When he'd created Prometheus under a previous presidential administration, he'd recruited only the best of the best for the teams, and I was his original hire, the first person to go through Prometheus Assessment and Selection. Kurt trusted my judgment, going so far as to allow Jennifer to attempt A&S as a female civilian when everyone else said he was crazy, and I trusted him as a commander. But that didn't mean I wouldn't fight him on Amena.

Like I said before, that was sort of my specialty. While we were closer than blood on the friendship front, when he wore the commander hat, I was more than willing to tell him he was full of shit—and I was one of the few who could get away with it.

Two minutes later I was pulling in behind a late-model rental car, our little drive now three-deep in vehicles. I exited, looked up, and saw Kurt Hale on my second-floor balcony, leaning on the rail and holding a beer. He said, "Running errands for the partner. How domesticated."

I smiled, reached in to grab the two small bags I had, and said, "Yeah, well, it pretty much ended in failure. I'll be right up."

A minute later I'd given my bags to Jennifer. Kurt was still on the balcony with the door closed. She said, "He's going to take Amena. That's why he's here. He pulled all those strings with the Oversight Council, and now he has to make it good."

The Oversight Council was the board that oversaw all Project Prometheus activities, which included my team. Nobody ever mentioned the program name out loud, calling everyone associated with it an innocuous nickname: the Taskforce. While GRS was doing pretty well on the commercial front—enough to let us buy this house—it's primary purpose was as a cover to allow penetration of denied areas for one reason: to drive a stake into the heart of threats that could affect US national interests.

I knew the Council was not happy with my decision to bring Amena to the United States because it had caused too many questions about how she jumped the line, potentially exposing the cover of GRS. How does a barely there company bring home a refugee and pass through customs and immigration without a hitch? The answer was because I had some people on my side, very important people who'd greased the skids. And that was making the Oversight Council nervous, since it would take only one thread to unwind the GRS cover, which would then unwind Project Prometheus and jeopardize the careers of anyone associated with it. Because Project Prometheus was decidedly illegal. An extrajudicial killing machine that was sanctioned at the highest level.

I passed Jennifer the bags and said, "I couldn't find the damn cheese you wanted."

Amena came up, pointed at the balcony, and said, "Why is he here? Is it me?"

She was like an animal that could smell a threat, having lived on the edge of survival for much of her short life. I looked at her and saw the pain of losing the first bit of sanctuary she'd ever experienced. And I realized I didn't want her to leave. For the first time in close to a decade—really since the loss of my family—I was content with my life, and I wanted that feeling to remain.

I brushed her cheek and said, "Don't worry about it. At least for this trip."

"Promise?"

I said, "Yes, doodlebug. I promise."

Jennifer heard me use the nickname that was once my daughter's and smiled. Amena relaxed. I turned to Jennifer, saying, "Just keep getting ready. I'll see what's up."

I grabbed a couple of beers and exited onto my upper balcony. I shook Kurt's hand, handed him another beer, and he said, "I hear Kylie is your new nanny."

I said, "I guess that depends. What's up with the sudden visit?"

He demurred, saying, "Looks like GRS is making more money than I remembered. This is a pretty nice house."

Which wasn't really true. It was an old row house that required enormous maintenance against plumbing leaks, pests, and electrical problems, but it *was* on the peninsula of Charleston, which was pretty cool.

I said, "So you want to cut my pay? Is that it? Because the Taskforce doesn't pay me nearly what I'm worth. I get a fortune helping some university do nothing more than excavate a dig. Shit, the last three jobs I did bought this house. I get peanuts from you dodging bullets."

He laughed and said, "I should have never let you two go find that temple in Guatemala. I've never heard the end of it."

"You never would have had GRS without it. We're the deepest cover organization you have."

He turned serious and said, "What's the status with Brazil?"

I said, "We've got the contract locked in with the university for the Jesuit UNESCO site, and it's a stone's throw from the triple frontier. Easy for us to work there and penetrate the area."

The triple frontier—or tri-border region—was the juncture of the borders of Argentina, Brazil, and Paraguay, a Wild West area heavy with Hezbollah activity. GRS always had to have a reason for operating, and we'd found one in the Rio Grande do Sul state in southern Brazil, an ancient Jesuit church called São Miguel das Missões that was slowly falling apart. A university, in coordination with the United Nations, wanted to stop the passage of time, and they'd hired us to help facilitate. Which was perfect, because we were going to use it to put some Hezbollah heads on a spike.

Kurt said, "Sounds like it's tracking."

"It is. Knuckles and Brett are already down there, prepping the battlefield. They head to Salvador in a couple of days, and Jennifer and I will link up with them there. But you know that. You're the one who fought to keep them on my team."

I was unique in the Taskforce in that I was a pure civilian now. Brett was a paramilitary member of the CIA and Knuckles was in the Navy. It had been a fight to allow me—now a civilian—to be the team leader of active-duty guys, but neither Brett nor Knuckles would have it any other way. We were a family that had bled together when *I* was on active duty, and while others in the government fought the decision on purely bureaucratic grounds, Kurt understood what teamwork meant.

In the end, the Taskforce was a strange beast, and it was just one more permutation from the norm. Kurt Hale had fought for me, and I'd regained my leadership position after I'd left active duty. After I'd crawled out of the abyss.

He just nodded, and I could tell he was thinking about something else.

I said, "Okay, sir, what's the point of this visit? It isn't our trip to Brazil, because you see those SITREPs. Just get it out."

He sighed, then looked at me, saying, "The Council has found a place for Amena. But you're not going to like it."

"What's that mean?"

"They want to repatriate her into the system. Put her into the refugee flow back in Syria."

He saw my face and said, "Wait, wait, she won't be put back into danger. She'll just be placed in a camp outside of Syria, either Jordan or Lebanon, and she'll get preferential treatment. She'll be back here in a year, maybe less."

I looked at him and said, "Are you fucking serious? Is that what *you* would do?"

He frowned and said, "Pike, there is more at risk here than her. I'm trying to do the best thing for her, but you short-circuited that. Don't blame me. *You're* the one who brought her here on a covert aircraft after a covert mission. It's hard to explain."

I leaned back and said, "So she's not worth the destruction she will cause if anyone makes the connection."

He nodded and said, "That's about it. I'm here on behalf of the Oversight Council. They wanted to jerk her ass outright. I told them to hold off."

I said, "How much time do I have?"

"What? You have no time. This is it."

"Bullshit. I'm going to Brazil in the next few days. How much time can you get me?"

"What do you mean?"

"Let me get this mission done first. Give me some time to cushion the blow. Don't take her tomorrow. Sell it as 'Pike's gone on a Taskforce mission. Can't take her now.' How hard is that?"

He said, "I don't know if I can do that."

I said, "Sir, I'm asking. I have never asked before. Give me this. I've given you my blood. *She's* given you *her* blood. All I'm asking is for a trip. Fuck those assholes in the Oversight Council."

He nodded, not looking at me. He said, "Okay, Pike. I'm with you. I'll delay it, but it's going to happen. You need to get your head around that."

I said, "I'll get my head around it when I need to. She's not going back to Syria. That's the end of it. Fuck the Oversight Council."

He looked at me to see if I was serious, and Jennifer came out on the balcony, saying, "Pike, I have to go back to the store. You didn't get everything I needed."

She'd clearly heard what I'd said and was trying to defuse the situation. And it worked. Kurt and I stared at each other for a beat, then he said, "I'll go. You guys stay here."

I said, "Sir, you don't want to try to find what she's making. It's impossible."

He laughed and said, "Not everyone is a Neanderthal. Let me go. You guys need to talk."

He walked back into the house, and Jennifer looked at me. I shook my head. Amena peered at me behind the door, and I felt crushed. All I'd done was give her hope, and now that was going to be devastated.

Jennifer followed behind him, and I could see her giving him instructions on what to buy, the things that I'd missed. I watched him go down the stairs, and then saw him appear below me. He looked up and said, "I can't get out."

I said, "Take my Jeep."

I tossed the keys down, and he caught them, looked at the Jeep, and said, "This is probably the biggest risk I've taken since I was running shotgun with you in Iraq."

I laughed and said, "And I kept you alive then."

He crawled into my CJ-7, stuck in the key, turned the ignition, and an explosion erupted, shredding his life in a fireball that turned the Jeep into a shrapnel blast of flying parts.

I was thrown back, feeling the shock wave of the explosion and dully hearing the tinkling of auto parts spackling the roof.

I sat up, staring in shock at the inferno below me, the Jeep burning furiously. It made no sense. I couldn't get my mind around it. I saw the body in the driver's seat, slumped over with its hair on fire, an arm dangling outside the door by a piece of tendon still connected to the shoulder, and felt a helplessness. I placed my hands on the railing and began to squeeze, a white-hot rage coursing through my body.

Kurt Hale was my mentor, my protector, and the man I always wanted to emulate. The one man I had always wanted to be. He had been family, and now he was dead. Because of me.

Because I was the target.

About the Author

BRAD TAYLOR was born on Okinawa, Japan, but grew up on 40 acres in rural Texas. Graduating from the University of Texas, he was commissioned as a second lieutenant in the U.S. Army Infantry. Brad served for more than 21 years, retiring as a Special Forces Lieutenant Colonel. He holds a Master's of Science in Defense Analysis from the Naval Postgraduate School, with a concentration in Irregular Warfare. When not writing, he serves as a security consultant on asymmetric threats for various agencies. He lives in Charleston, SC, with his wife and two daughters.

Discover great authors, exclusive offers, and more at hc.com.